Kenzie was high on adrenaline until Angelo tugged her inside...

"Are you crazy?" He put his hands on her shoulders and pressured her into a chair.

"What are you doing? I know who the poacher is. You know I do. I just have to find where he anchors, and then I can turn him in myself."

"You think you know, but you're wrong."

"You just moved here about two minutes ago. How can you know anything?"

"I'll tell you how." She sprang off the chair, hands on her hips. "I met Jigs, and he's a very nice man, and his dog is gentle and sweet."

"You met him? Right. When? Where?"

"Yesterday, at the flea market. I had a nice long conversation with him."

Angelo backed away as if he might catch her disease. "*Holy ship*, Red. You have lost your mind. Stay away from him. Jigs is a killer and a lowlife lobster thief. And that mutt of his is just as mean."

"Children, children." Father Murphy hurried toward them. "What is all this about?"

"I'm trying to explain to her that"—Angelo glanced at Father Murphy and softened his tone—"just because someone is nice to her doesn't mean she can trust him."

"But Jigs is a nice man."

"I'm telling you, Jigs is a thief and worse."

"Jigs?" The lines on Father's forehead deepened. "A thief? As far as I know, there's one Jigs on this island, and she's a dog."

ISLAND
STING

Bonnie J. Doerr

leap

Island Sting
COPYRIGHT © 2010 by Bonnie J. Doerr

Previously published as *Kenzie's Key* by Laurel & Herbert, Inc., 2003. Present edition has been revised significantly.

Contact Information: info@leapbks.com

Cover Art by *Leap Books*
Interior Art by *Joanna Britt*
Maps by *Laurie Edwards*

Leap Books
Powell, WY
www.leapbks.com

Publishing History
First Leap Edition 2010
ISBN: 978-1-61603-002-5

LCCN 2009941501

Published in the United States of America

DEDICATION

To green teens everywhere

Acknowledgements

Thanks to the talented Piedmont Plotters:
The eagle-eyed Nicole Corbett, Laurie Edwards,
Bernadette Hearne, Maggie Moe, and Joyce
Potter
Without them, Island Sting would not exist.

To Oh! Franklin Dukes for his unconditional
patience and encouragement

To Edgardo Alvarado-Vazquez, foreign language
professor extraordinaire; Joan Campion for her
comprehensive reading; Joan Langley for her
discerning eye; Vicki Weeks for her generous
input; Monroe County (Florida) Commissioner
Sylvia Murphy for sharing her time and
memories; and
Sanford Brown and the rest of the staff at the
National Key Deer Refuge for guidance and
information

Inexpressible gratitude for the perseverance and
wisdom of my amazing editor, Kat O'Shea

Praise for Island Sting

"Island Sting is a fast-paced, environmental thriller that teens will tear into. Once you start reading, you'll find yourself flipping pages as fast as you can, eager to find out what happens next. Great action, great characters, and a message that will resonate with readers of all ages."

~**Frances O'Roark Dowell**, Edgar-award-winning author of *Dovey Coe, Chicken Boy*, and *Shooting the Moon*

"Impetuous Kenzie, dashing Angel, and a fascinating cast of four-legged characters make green go down easy in this fast-paced eco-mystery."

~**Louise Hawes**, award-winning author of *Black Pearls, Waiting for Christopher*, and *Rosey in the Present Tense*

"As Kenzie's feelings became my own, I didn't want to put this book down. It was as if I was Kenzie. I wanted to get up and go clean up litter and catch that rude poacher. But then I remembered all that's tough to do with a book in your hand."

~**Jenna Hoglander**, West Forsyth High School

Bonnie Doerr has done it again! Her story of ecology and intrigue on Big Pine Key should appeal to teens as well as adults who enjoy a good yarn that includes romance and poachers and at the same time gently teaches valuable lessons about preserving our wildlife.

As a resident and refuge volunteer, I found that the book's factual basis was accurate, and her descriptive writing put me at the scene so that I also enjoyed her fictional story. Although the protagonist is a girl, there are enough supporting male players to hold a boy's interest as well. Highly recommended.

~Sandy (Sanford) Brown,
National Key Deer Refuge volunteer
Big Pine Key, FL

For teen readers, Kenzie rushes into excitement, rescuing a miniature Key deer from near drowning, chasing poachers, and, along the way, learning about herself. Having recently moved to Big Pine Key, Florida, she faces both a new environment and new friends with equal energy and enthusiasm.

For environmentalists, Kenzie's many new friends teach her about the endangered and threatened flora and fauna of the Florida Keys as she encounters, among other species, Key deer, poisonwood, and hawksbill turtles. Kenzie quickly realizes this fragile environment needs her help, too

~Susan M. Nugent,
author of *Women Conserving the Florida Keys*

DRIVE WITH CAUTION
YOU ARE ENTERING AN
ENDANGERED SPECIES AREA

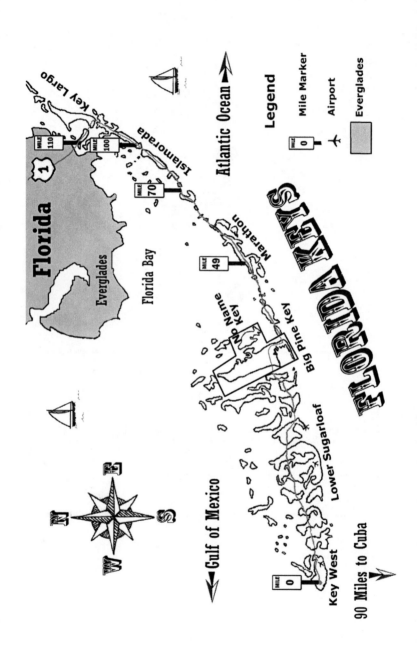

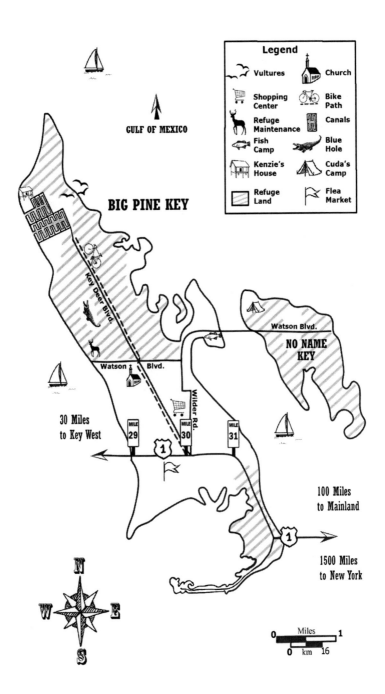

Chapter 1

Splash!

Ripples circled across the dark water farther down the canal. Kenzie scrambled through the mangrove thicket, stumbling over tangled roots toward the disturbance. Branches caught her hair and scratched her face. When she thought she'd reached the spot, she crept to the water's edge, but the surface was calm. Had she miscalculated?

No. There. Something broke the surface. It swam in jerky circles. Round and round. Over and over. She shielded her eyes from the sun. A long nose cut through the water, leaving a little wake in its path. It circled closer. Nose, two eyes, and long ears.

A dog!

It paddled away, floundered, and went under.

Kenzie tripped along the rugged canal desperate to save it. Every step of the way, she struggled with the image of Scruffy bolting from the Jeep at that gas station—chasing that scrawny cat. The speeding red Corvette. Why hadn't she put Scruffy on his leash? Why? Oh God, that thump. That howl.

Tears flooded her eyes. She had to save *this* dog.

How? If she jumped in, she'd never get out. Sheer rock walls. Too steep. Too high.

"Help!" she screamed. "Somebody, anybody, help!"

A limb. She needed a long limb with lots of branches. He could prop his front legs on it.

Kenzie ducked under a silver-leafed tree and emerged near the struggling animal. "Swim, little guy. Don't give up." She stumbled. Reached for a branch.

The ground collapsed.

Splash!

She plunged into the canal.

Splatter. Splat.

A landslide of gravel tumbled after her.

Chapter 2

DOWN. DOWN. DOWN. So far down.

Don't panic. Relax. It's only water.
"*Kick!*" Her coach's voice echoed in her brain. "*Kick, ladies. Kick!*"

Kenzie burst to the surface. Gasped and spun. Ow! Her eyes. She blinked. They still stung. She distinguished the dog's long nose in the blur. There! Ouch! She blinked again. Still burning. She had to keep her eyes shut. But shadowy images of a dying Scruffy merged with those of the drowning animal. *This* dog would live.

Adrenaline rushed through her, fired by grief and guilt. She dug deep. Powered her strokes toward the puffing dog. She had to reach it before it went under again. "I'm coming, fella. Almost there."

His frantic snorts grew louder. She had to be close. Her next stroke landed on his long ears. She slid her hand down his neck. A collar. Yes! She grabbed it—a victorious snatch in the playoffs.

Terrified bleating pierced the air. What the...? Its thrashing feet whacked her. A hard wallop for doggie paws. She chanced a look. It lunged and splashed. *Yikes*. She closed her eyes. Too late. That settled it. She would not open her eyes again, but she *would* hold tight to this collar.

Kenzie concentrated. What now? Keeping him afloat was no problem. In class, she'd always been the one to demonstrate pulling a panicked swimmer to safety. How to get out of the canal was the problem. No way could she make it back to the ladder on the dock. Start swimming.

Kick, stroke, pull.
Swim to the bank.
Kick, stroke, pull.
Grab a root.
Kick, stroke, pull.
Yell for help.
Kick, stroke, slap.

5

The wall. Kenzie moved along the sharp coral rock, handhold by handhold, until she felt a root. She tugged to test its strength. Satisfied, she hung on, treading water and bobbing like a buoy on a mooring.

"Help! I can't get out of the canal. Help!"

No response. Mom was too far away to hear. Most other houses were shuttered for the season. Was *anyone* around?

The exhausted animal no longer gave her trouble, but the root was slimy. Her hand slipped. Her head went under. She scissor kicked, popped up, and treaded water. Was there another handhold? *Don't sting. Don't sting.* She opened her eyes. Owie! Burning fog. She jammed them shut. Groped and found a more secure root.

"Help! Please, help!" Muffled words through waterlogged ears. *Louder.* "Help!"

A voice. Was someone coming?

"Suumm aatch." Garbled words.

She whipped her head back and forth to clear her ears. Concentrated. "Is somebody up there?"

"Yup."

Thank you, God. "What'd you say?"

"Some catch. Never caught anything this big."

"Please, get us out of here."

6

"Grab the net. I'll fish you out."

Kenzie sputtered. "What net? I can't see."

"So, open your eyes. Go for it. You gotta let go of that root."

"We'll go under."

"No, you won't. The net's right in front of you. Look."

"No. When I open my eyes they burn like crazy. Like I'll go blind."

"It's the salt water. Grab the net. Hold on to the deer. I'll pull you both to the ramp."

What? Her ears must be clogged again. Hold on to what? The net. He said to grab the net. She cracked her eyes. Ignored the burn, aimed, closed her eyes again, and lunged for the net. Success!

"Ready? Here we go."

She swished through the water like a rag mop over a floor, the dog a heavy drag. Her arms ached.

"We're almost there. You can make it."

Her grip weakened. Fingers slipped. *No.* She lost the net. How much longer could she hold the dog's collar?

"It's okay. You can touch bottom here."

Please, be right. Kenzie relaxed her legs. She did it. She touched bottom. When she stood, her head and shoulders were out of the water. Bliss.

"Open your eyes. They won't burn long. Help me get the deer out of the water."

Help him get the *what*?

"Come on. It'll get hypothermia if it's not already dead."

Dead? *He can't die.* Kenzie let go of the collar and eased the animal toward the voice. She would not lose another dog. No way!

"Okay. Got her. Come on out."

Burn or no burn, it was time to suck it up. Kenzie blinked non-stop as she walked and dripped her way up the concrete incline. The stinging eased a bit, but as her vision cleared she couldn't believe what came into focus. The bedraggled animal stretched out on the boat ramp was a soggy, exhausted, very small deer. A deer wearing a blue collar. A collar with a numbered tag attached to it. "That's not a dog."

"No kidding."

He was about her age. *Nice.* He'd sounded older.

He crouched next to the deer. Wavy, dark hair fell across his bronzed, rock-star face.

Oh— Geesh— St. Joe's Girls' Academy hadn't prepared her for anything like this. *He—* Why wouldn't her heart settle down? He was— He was so—talking. He was talking to her. *Shake it off, Kenzie.*

His fingers stroked the deer's side. "She's in bad shape. This girl's lucky I was over here bait fishing."

The deer wasn't the only lucky girl. For a fleeting moment her spirits lightened. Maybe Mom had been right about these islands being Paradise.

When he looked up at Kenzie, his dark eyes flashed.

Was he angry with her? She *had* been silly about the saltwater thing. The dog comment sounded wacko too.

"I'll carry her to my boat and go for help."

"No. Take her to the first house. My mom's there. She's a nurse. She'll know what to do."

He looked at her like he questioned her sanity. "Guess it would be faster." He gathered the dripping, limp body in his strong, brown arms.

Kenzie followed, squeezing water out of her hair and lifting sections of wet shirt off her sticky skin. A tiny piece of her envied the deer. *Yikes.* She tripped on a pile of orange plastic webbing, bumped into his shoulder, and wanted to die.

What a klutz. "Somebody should clean up this pile of junk."

"That's not junk. It's a weed guard for the boat ramp. I took it down when I pulled you out."

Weed guard? It could wait. She wasn't opening her mouth again.

He shifted the doe's weight and trudged up to the road. The miniature deer's head lolled on his shoulder. Kenzie sloshed behind on quivering jelly legs.

They neared the house, and Kenzie moved ahead to open the gate. She led him up the fifteen stairs to the screened porch. In the living room, her mother paced back and forth, phone to her ear.

"Yes, Nana. We arrived a little while ago. I don't know. She must be off exploring. Yes, everything's fine with the house, but we had a horrible accident along the way with Scruffy—"

"Mom!"

"What in the world?" Her mother rushed out on the porch. "Nana, I have to go. Kenzie is— she's—I'll call back."

"Mom, we need your help."

"Where have you been?" Her mother grappled with a series of facial expressions. "You're sopping wet. What on earth happened? Look at you."

"Mother, look at the deer. Not me. It might be dying. Please do something!"

Her mother rubbed her forehead, then tossed the phone on a wicker table. "Okay. Let's take a look." She lifted boxes off the lounge chair. "Kenzie, the towels are in one of those boxes. Grab some. Put the poor thing down here, please. Its head at the low end."

The rescuer touched his face to the tiny deer's neck, then moved toward the chair. He held her head close and knelt. Leaning forward he lowered her hindquarters until they touched the lounge. Then inch by inch he lowered and positioned her chest and head.

Her mother held her lips to the doe's nose. "It's not—" She placed her fingers on the inside of the doe's dainty back leg. "Wait. There's a faint pulse. Maybe I could..." She looked up at Kenzie. "Oh boy, I've never ventilated a deer before, but why not? Kenzie, help me lay the little thing on its right side. Easy now."

She opened the deer's mouth and pulled its tongue forward. Next she covered its nose and mouth with her own mouth and blew little puffs of air into its nostrils. Amazingly, the tiny chest rose. She puffed again. Once more the chest rose.

Kenzie counted off one, two, three, four seconds for every puff her mother made. The little chest continued to rise and fall. But when her mother stopped the rhythmic puffing, the little deer's chest stopped moving. She checked for a pulse again.

"Kenzie," her mother commanded, "you're going to have to help me. Now." She positioned Kenzie's fingers and thumbs on the deer's chest near the bend in its front legs. "Press here firmly, but gently, six times for every puff of air I blow."

Her mom puffed. Kenzie pressed. Over and over until, at last, the little deer gurgled and coughed. Her coughs became nonstop quivers, and her huge, brown eyes cleared and brightened.

Kenzie's teary eyes met her mother's shining ones. They reached for each other's hands and turned to include the mysterious rescuer in their wonder, but the porch was empty.

Chapter 3

IMAGES OF THE GORGEOUS STRANGER haunted Kenzie the whole time she was in the shower. A happy distraction from the mold and mildew on the old tile walls. But what were the chances she'd ever see him again? Zero to none. He'd come by boat. He could live anywhere in these islands. He was history. She'd put him in her overflowing get-over-it basket. Scrubbing off the sticky salt water didn't wash away his memory. It worked him under her skin instead.

She stepped out of the stall and sniffed. Pizza! Satisfying her empty stomach would take things off her overwhelmed mind. For a while.

In Nana's linen closet, she found a musty towel. Kenzie wrapped her head in it, then dressed in clothes from her overnight bag. She walked around more stacked cartons Mom had carried up, and went to check on the deer. The doe hadn't budged.

The phone rang. Her mom answered. Immediately, she moved it away from her ear.

Uh-oh. That was Nana's frustrated rapid-fire tone. Kenzie stayed out of the way as her mother paced in frustration.

"I can't keep an eye on her every second, Mother. She's not a baby."

Why was Nana giving Mom such a hard time?

Her mother stomped the floor. "That does not make me an irresponsible parent!"

Kenzie touched her mom's shoulder and reached for the phone. "I'll explain to Nana."

But her mother hung up, then snapped at Kenzie—a skill she'd perfected over the past several weeks. "I told you not to go wandering off. It's the first thing I said. Your escapade is a perfect example of why I was hesitant to take the position down here. If Nana hadn't offered this house rent free, I wouldn't have."

Thanks for nothing, Nana.

"This neighborhood is too remote and wild. And you're so—"

Here it comes.

"—so impulsive. I can't trust you to be the

least bit careful. Don't you ever think before you act?"

Impulsive, thoughtless, careless, irresponsible. Over the last few weeks, Kenzie had been labeled them all.

Her mom's eyes fired blue icicles. "It's enough that I have to worry about how to make a living now that your father's left us. I don't have enough energy to worry about you and what you're getting into." She flipped open boxes, one after another, peered in, then smacked the tops shut again.

Kenzie backed out of her mom's way. Did she even know what she was looking for?

Her mother knocked over a lamp, picked it up, and kept on going. "We know nothing about this place or its people. There's a prison right down the road. Murderers and thieves could be living out there in the woods or on those old beat-up boats out in the bay." She pointed through the screen porch toward some invisible water.

"Mom, lighten up."

"I can't lighten up. I don't like the looks of half of the people I saw at the store. Not one clean-shaven or decently dressed man. I never saw so many tattoos on young people. And children with dreadlocks. Dreadlocks!"

15

Kenzie hid her grin. She couldn't remember seeing any tattoos or children in dreads. But that would be more interesting than all the uniforms and copycat kids she was used to seeing.

"A lot of those people looked like, well... This place is... It's uncivilized." Her mom swept a pile of clothes off a chair and collapsed, rubbing her eyes.

Obviously, her mother had changed her mind about Paradise. "Mother, what store were you in? Daze Mart?"

"Kenzie, you can't imagine what went through my mind when I saw you coming up the stairs, looking like you did, with that strange boy. If you'd stayed here to help me unload like I told you, nothing would have happened to you. Oh, honey, you could have drowned!"

"Mom, if I'd stayed here, the deer would have drowned!" Kenzie whipped the towel off her head and smacked it on a box. *Thwap.* "All you care about is yourself. *You* needed help unloading. *You* didn't want to be worried. What about the deer? What about me?"

Kenzie swatted at the mosquitoes buzzing her ears. "Do you think I wanted to leave my friends, my teammates, St. Joe's, everything I've ever known to come to this crappy place? Do you think I wanted to drive to a mosquito-infested island at the end of the entire continent? That I wanted to—to—let Scruffy get killed!" She sank to the floor, sobbing and shaking.

Her mother's eyes filled. She eased herself from the chair to the floor. "Oh, Kenzie, I'm so sorry, baby. Let's not yell at each other. It's the last thing we need."

She scooted closer to Kenzie and softened her tone. "What happened to Scruffy was worse than horrid. It'll be a long time before either one of us gets over it. We're both going to miss him terribly." She pulled Kenzie's damp towel off the box, then touched it to Kenzie's eyes. "Like right now. He'd be all over our laps, wiggling and kissing us. It was impossible to stay angry when Scruffy was around. Baby, I'm not angry with you anyway. I'm angry at the mess we're in."

She untangled Kenzie's wet curls with her fingers. "It's been one exhausting, nightmare of a drive. My back hurts like the devil. I'm tired... and scared."

Kenzie wiped her face with the cloth. "Me too, Mom."

"You're not scared. It was a brave and wonderful thing you did when you jumped in the canal to save that deer. I'm proud of you, honey."

"But, Mom—" Kenzie lifted her face. "I didn't jump in. I fell in. I couldn't see, and all the time I thought it was a dog. I can be so stupid."

"Stupid? Don't you ever say that again. Strong and brave is more like it. Fell or jumped. Dog or deer. Who cares? You saved a life. That's what counts."

Kenzie sniffed and rubbed her eyes. "Actually, Mom, we saved it, you and me, and the mystery boy. We don't know where he came from or where he went. We don't even know his name."

Tap. Tap.

"Ah—ahem."

Someone at the screen door?

Tap. Tap.

"Do you mean me?"

Kenzie's heart skipped. *He's here.* Standing in the shadows on the top step.

"My name's Angelo."

Had she conjured him? How long had he been there?

Kenzie's mom poked her.

"Oh, hi!" Kenzie wiped her eyes on her sleeves, jumped up, then flipped on the porch light. "Come on in." She opened the screen door.

"So, what's *your* name?" he asked.

"Kenzie."

"I'm Margaret Ryan." Her mom pushed herself up off the floor. "We were talking about you, wondering where you'd disappeared to. Sit down if you can find a spot. You're just in time. I was about to take dinner out of the oven."

"So, Kenzie," he said, "the deer hasn't left the chair. How's she doing?"

"She seems okay. But I don't know how to take care of her. I don't even know what she eats. Or if she needs vaccines or flea and tick medicine. I can't believe I found her. My dog died, and now I have a deer. Is this good karma or what?"

Angelo stared at her like she'd sprouted antennae. Better explain. "See, with those big soft brown eyes she reminds me of Scruffy, and a while ago she nuzzled my hand like he used to do."

Why wasn't he saying anything? Maybe she wasn't asking the right questions.

"Where do you think she came from? Can we find out whose pet she is?"

Still nothing.

"How do you think she got into the canal? Maybe she fell off a boat."

"Whoa, slow down!" Angelo held up his hand and backed up like he wanted to escape. "You don't know about these deer, do you?"

"Well, they're super small. But I'm guessing there's more."

"Yeah. A lot more. Look, I'm sorry about your dog. But you can't keep that deer. And a deer falling off a boat? Unreal. Now I know you're a tourist."

He walked over, pressed the top of a box marked *Books*, then sat on it. "You know, most tourists come to the Keys and swim with fish or dolphins, not deer."

"We're not tourists." She picked up a pile of her mother's scrubs. "Mom works at the hospital. We live here." Kenzie put the clothes down. Why was she making such a big deal of this? She truly wished they were visiting.

"You live here?" Angelo looked around the room full of boxes. "Yeah, right. You've been here how many hours? You won't last long. You'll leave like everyone else."

"Well, we're not like everyone else." Kenzie propped her hands on her hips. "Why can't I keep the deer? I won't let her fall in the canal like her last owner."

"She didn't have an owner."

"But she's wearing a collar."

Her mother patted a barstool. "Sweetie, sit

down. Relax."

Kenzie ignored her. She glared at Angelo.

"It's a research collar," Angelo said. "What do you think that tag with the number 77 on it is? A charm or something? It's her identification number so the scientists can keep stats on her. She's a Florida Key deer. An endangered species. Didn't you learn about them in your New York school?"

Wow. This sure put things in a new perspective.

Kenzie slumped on the stool. "You're serious?"

"Yup. They don't live anywhere else in the world."

"An endangered species. That is so cool. How'd you know we're from New York anyway?"

"Your Jeep's got license plates, right?"

Kenzie chewed on her hair. She should have thought of that.

"So, anyway, about the deer," he continued. "It's illegal to keep them as pets. It's even illegal to feed them. And if you keep her—" He grinned. In a deep radio voice, he announced, "Welcome to Paradise. Spend your first week on us free—in the county jail!"

Her mom placed the steaming pizza on the counter. "So, if we can't feed the little deer, I guess that means more for us. Come on over, Angelo. Dig in."

"No problem. I'm easy." Angelo leaned on the counter. "Anyway, she didn't fall into the canal. I have a solid idea how she got there." No longer teasing, he sounded downright menacing.

Kenzie's mom put sodas on the counter. "Really? How?" She pulled a folding chair over, then sat waiting.

Kenzie allowed him two bites before she burst out, "Angelo! How did she get in the canal?"

He swallowed. "Okay. It's like this. There's a weird old sponger around here everybody calls Jigs. He lives on an ancient houseboat. Moves it all the time. You never know where he's anchored, and you never know what he's doing. I trust him like a barracuda."

"See, Kenzie. I warned you."

"Mom, shhh. Please. Keep going, Angelo."

Angelo kept eating.

Kenzie sighed. Full volume. "What about

Jigs?"

He pulled a lead fishing weight from his shirt pocket, then rolled it back and forth on the countertop, as if it helped him spin his words.

"I'm pretty sure he robs Dad's lobster and crab traps. A couple times this past season, I saw Jigs' red runabout near traps at Dad's best spot. After that boat's been there, those traps come up empty. Every time."

"What do lobster and crab traps have to do with deer?" Kenzie said.

"He's got a thing for traps. On land or in water. Uses old metal ones for deer when he doesn't shoot 'em first. There're no lobster or crab traps out now, so he's got plenty of time to poach deer. He hunts with a mangy old hound."

"I understand how someone could make money selling crabs and lobster," Kenzie's mom said. "That would be a reason to rob traps. But is there a market for venison?"

"Not really, there's not enough meat on Key deer." He wiped his mouth. "Guess Jigs is mean enough to think it's sport."

"That's sick." Kenzie dropped her pizza slice in mid-bite. "And disgusting. So, back to the canal. Did he toss her in?"

"No, it was his dog." Angelo slurped his soda.

"Dogs can panic deer. Make them stampede. If they head toward a canal and can't stop in time... Hey, you saw what happens. I'm sure that old poacher and his hound chased that deer down." Angelo's eyes stormed. "Deer can swim, but if they can't get out, well—"

Kenzie swallowed. "She was lucky you were there."

"You're the one who saved her. She couldn't get out of this canal because of that weed guard. It was stretched across the ramp at water level to keep the seaweed off the ramp. She'd have drowned if you hadn't found her. It wouldn't be the first time it happened." He cocked his head. "What's that scratching sound?"

They tiptoed toward the screened porch. The doe was struggling to get off the lounge chair.

"Do you think she's hungry?" Kenzie eased forward.

Angelo stopped in the doorway. "Maybe, but she's going to have trouble getting anything. She can't seem to put much weight on her front legs."

Kenzie's mom peeked around his shoulder. "You're right. And I think my patient needs a bathroom break."

"I'll take her out." Angelo lifted the miniature deer. "She doesn't weigh much more than thirty-

five pounds. She needs to eat."

Kenzie followed Angelo as he carried the quaking deer down the steps. Slowly, he stooped to release her. The tiny, weak doe balanced on three spindly legs, refusing to rest any weight on her left front hoof.

"Like I said, she needs food. I'll get some red mangrove branches. Deer love their leaves." Angelo headed toward the thicket beyond the fence.

The little deer hobbled around the barren yard until she relieved herself, dropping a little pile of dark pellets. Angelo returned with food, but no amount of encouragement tempted the doe to eat.

"I think it's best for her to stay outside tonight," Kenzie's mom called from the porch. "Maybe she'll eat if we leave her alone."

"But, Mom, she can't take care of herself. She's hurt and weak. What if there're dogs around?"

Her mother started down the steps. "She can't get out of the fence, Kenzie, and dogs can't get in. She's not used to being in a house. She'll be more comfortable outdoors. See, she's settling down in that pile of leaves under the steps."

The deer's large ears twitched as a rattling

vehicle approached. A well-used pickup came into view.

"That's my dad. He dropped me off on his way to look at a motor. I better go. He needs to crash so he can get up early to repair his traps."

"Wait," Kenzie said. "I forgot to ask. Why'd you disappear so fast?"

"You guys were busy when I noticed the sun was low. I was running out of time and had to—"

"What? Are you a vampire?"

"The tide was going down. That's what. My boat can't make it through the cut at low tide. I'd get stuck over here. Spending the night on a sandbar with a zillion mosquitoes is no fun."

"Did you get through without any trouble?" Kenzie's mom asked.

"Scraped bottom once. Not bad." He eyed Kenzie. "Contact the refuge in the morning. Someone will come get the deer."

The truck stopped across the street. Angelo's dad beeped the horn and called to Angelo in a flurry of Spanish. Among the unfamiliar words, she heard, "Anthill! Anthill!"

"Thanks for the pizza, Ms. Ryan." Angelo took off, and the gate slammed behind him.

Anthills? She'd read about Florida's fire ant

problem, but never imagined they'd made it to the Keys. *Great.* This morning she'd arrived heartbroken on this weird island. Risked her life to rescue an endangered deer. Learned she couldn't keep it. And now she had to worry about killer ants. *Welcome to Paradise.*

Overwhelmed with fatigue, Kenzie and her mother cleaned up the counter. Too tired for conversation, they dug sheets and pillows out of cartons, tossed them on the beds, and collapsed.

Hours later, heart beating like a jungle drum, Kenzie awoke. She'd been screaming, fleeing a pack of barking wild dogs. Those barks were part of the dream, weren't they? Better check on the deer.

Kenzie slipped on sandals, found her flashlight, then tiptoed through the house to the front steps. Halfway down, she stopped to shine her light between the stairs. The little pile of mangrove leaves was gone. The doe must have eaten. She was no longer under the house, so she was strong enough to move around. All good news.

Kenzie leaned over the railing. She flashed the light on the front yard. No deer. Next, she walked toward the canal. Where was the doe? Suddenly, it hit her. The side fencing ended at the water's edge. The canal was unprotected. Kenzie ran to the dock. Swept her light the length of the canal. No sign of the deer in the canal or yard.

No snorting, no splashing, nothing but the easy rattle of palm fronds in the breeze. She worked her way back toward the road, moving her flashlight beam along the fence, section by section until it illuminated the front gate.

The gate stood wide open.

Chapter 4

Kenzie searched up and down the block three times, behind houses, in the woods, and along the canal's edge. No deer. *Told you, Mom.* Anger built like a ticking bomb. She stomped up the front steps, knowing sleep was as lost as the deer.

In the pale light of dawn, Kenzie was armed and ready to battle. She slapped at mosquitoes and paced the front porch. The shower stopped running, the toilet flushed, and finally, her mother's bedroom radio blared.

Kenzie barged into her mom's room. "I wanted to keep the deer on the porch. But no. You said she'd be better off outside. Great idea, Mom. She's gone. The gate's wide open, and she's gone."

"Gone?" Her mother stopped tying her shoes.

Sat up straight. "How?"

"How do I know? Got any other super ideas? What if the poacher got her?" Kenzie tailgated her mom into the kitchen. "You've got to help me find her."

"Kenzie, I did what I thought was best. I didn't think she could get out." Her mom took a deep breath and ran her hands through her cropped hair. "I don't have time to look for her this morning. It's my first day at work." She picked up her bag and hoisted the strap over her shoulder. "I can't be late. I'm sorry, honey. I'm sure she's out looking for food."

"Yeah, right."

"I'll be back at four." Her mom shot Kenzie the Lockdown Look. "Don't you go searching for her either, young lady. I expect you to stay home and unpack."

Like this was home. Kenzie slumped onto a barstool.

Her mother scooped sugar into a travel mug. She banged the spoon back and forth, splashing the coffee. "I told you I was worried about people around here, and what Angelo said last night doesn't make me feel any better. Stay right here. This is not negotiable. Do you understand?" She snapped the lid down.

Kenzie sat on her crossed fingers. "Yes, Mother, I understand all right. Don't worry about me or the deer. You go off to work like everything is totally fine."

"I'm counting on you, Kenzie. You'll see. Everything *will* be fine." She rushed out the back door.

Right. Kenzie stuffed Scruffy's leash in her pocket. She grabbed a banana from the counter. As she ate, she watched the road across the canal through the kitchen window. The Jeep came into sight and disappeared. Kenzie bolted out the door and down the steps.

The deer couldn't have hobbled far on her shaky legs. Kenzie had to find the tiny thing before anything else happened to it. She needed to expand her search. If the deer was still alive, it would head for the safe forest across the canal. Kenzie raced across the bridge. *I will find you, Molly.*

Molly? The deer needed a name. But where had Molly come from? The *Titanic*? Of course. Unsinkable Molly Brown. It fit. The deer hadn't drowned. She wasn't going to get shot either. No way.

There had to be an opening in the edge of the dense undergrowth. *Yes.* A trail. Prickly branches grasped her clothes, caught her hair. She ducked and scrunched sideways as she squeezed along the deer trail.

Pop. Pop.

Kenzie jumped.

Rustle. Rustle.

She cringed.

A lizard scurried through the underbrush.

She sighed, then rounded a bend.

Snap. Crack.

Behind her. That was no lizard. Who—or what—was following her?

There. A tight thicket. Kenzie hid in a cocoon of shiny, droopy leaves. She worked her head between them. Got a clear view of the path. Molly! *Unbelievable.* Molly was following her. Kenzie's heart raced to the deer. Her feet itched to go along. *No.* Don't spook her. Make sure she's okay.

Step by step, the doe eased along the overgrown trail, nibbling foliage as she came. No sign of a limp. She moved out of the shadows. Her collar was missing. How could Kenzie catch her?

A few yards away the deer stopped to forage. *Crud.* Too heavy. Not Molly. Kenzie stepped back into the trees.

Another deer appeared. Was this Molly? No. Three more followed. Still no Molly. All collarless. All too big, except for a spotted fawn no more than fifteen inches high. Scruffy's size.

Kenzie didn't move, and soon all the deer were dining on tender shrubs in front of her. A scene from *Wild Kingdom*. She could have touched the closest one. They chewed, rolling their jaws back and forth. Their two-toned tails flicked rhythmically, flashing black on top, white below. The largest deer's head shot up. It snorted. Had it caught her scent? With tails flagging high and white, the little herd trotted off. Beelining toward the main road.

Stop! Kenzie bit her tongue. *Don't scream.* They could panic. Stampede smack into traffic. An engine roared. Loud. Louder. Could she change their course? She ripped out of the trees. Bulldozed through the thicket.

No! A blood-red car. The fatal Corvette blazed through her memory. Brakes squealed. Dread seized her heart. Gravel popped. There had been no horrendous thump. The car pulled off the road. Its engine stopped. Kenzie's heart rebooted. She crept to the edge of the woods. As if hypnotized, all five deer stared at the red car. Safe.

The driver held something out to the deer. Luring them forward. The poacher?

Two bold deer strolled toward him. *Stay away!* She closed her eyes and willed her words into their large velvety ears. *Stay back!*

On the near side of the car, the passenger extended something out of the window. Sunlight reflected off its shiny surface. A gun? Hard to tell in the blinding sun.

Kenzie moved closer. Crouched behind a thatch palm. Why hadn't she worn her sunglasses?

Crackle. Crackle. Crinkle.

What was going on? She squinted as if restricting light would enhance her hearing.

In the passenger's hand, a flash of yellow and blue. A potato chip bag. They were rattling a potato chip bag. Unbelievable. Those idiots were trying to feed the deer potato chips.

But the idiots knew what they were doing. Crushing the snack bag rang a deer dinner bell. The three previously hesitant deer perked up and trotted to the red car. All five surrounded the car, stretching their necks to reach the treats.

Unreal. Angelo had made a big deal about feeding Molly. *No people food!* He'd said it over and over.

If Kenzie had known Molly liked potato chips, she could have fixed the little doe a feast. They had a huge bag at home. Then Molly wouldn't have run off to find food. *If that's what had really happened.* She had to find Molly before she got hit by a car, or worse.

Reassured these were tourists, not poachers, Kenzie returned to the woods and picked her way through the thicket until the deer path opened onto a sunny clearing.

Yikes.

She flinched. A giant winged shadow swooped across her path.

Whoosh!

Kenzie hit the dirt.

Whoosh! Whoosh!

Face down. Hands on head.

Air rushed. One huge bird. Wings flapped. Two. Another and another brushed by.

She peeked between her arms.

Swoosh!

Savage hooked beak.

Zoom!

Massive wings.

"Go away!" She covered her head again.

Not real. She squeezed her eyes closed. Nightmare. Nothing to hear. Nothing to see. Ten counts. Deep breaths. Another peek. She didn't see anything. She pushed off the ground. Maybe she had imagined it. One last look. Hands on head, she raised her eyes. Tried not to lift her face. High above, the large gray and black winged birds soared in circles, like graceful kites. Peaceful, but creepy.

"Stay there. Whatever you are, stay up there!"

A long-lost science lesson teased the edge of her memory. Something about nature's scavengers, nature's cleanup brigade. Vultures. Turkey buzzards. Full-face skyward, she called, "You're buzzards. You won't hurt me because you only eat—dead animals."

No, no. Not Molly. Please, God, don't let me screw up again. Don't let me be too late.

She raced across the clearing toward the soaring vultures. Several circled lower and lower. Some landed in the pine trees. A few had already settled to the earth.

"Go away! Get out of here!" With one hand, she picked up a stick, with the other, split off a branch. She charged, flailing the air with both weapons. "Eeeeyah!" Like an avenging warrior, she rushed the winged devils that had landed.

The vultures fixed their cold beady eyes on her as they hopped. Toward her.

Grrrrrr.

Were they growling?

Another raspy *grrr.*

They were. Kenzie froze.

Hisssssuh.

Hissing too.

"That's it. You don't scare me, you bloody, ugly, bald-headed creeps. Eeeeyah! Eeeeyah!"

Wap. Wap.

Kenzie thrashed the grass, the dirt, the sky.

Wap. Wap. Wap.

She swung, slashed, and screamed. Finally, the creatures flapped to the treetops. Waiting. Staring. Menacing.

Tense and sweaty, Kenzie crouched in the field to rest. Now what? They weren't leaving.

Their eyes.... Those naked, blood-red heads.... How could she go any closer? But she had to. She had to know what had attracted the vultures.

Deep breath. Go on now. She stepped long and slow like a child playing *Mother May I* and matched her steps to a reassuring chant. "Vultures won't touch me. They can't hurt me."

Step by step, she moved forward. "Vultures won't touch me. They can't—"

No! She sidestepped. Clutched her stomach. *Ugh, eck!*

A gory mess of skin, hooves, and hair.

Chapter 5

Kenzie doubled over. Her banana breakfast rolled up her throat and spilled out. Missed her sneakers by a fraction. She ran from the carnage, then fell to her knees.

Too late. Oh, Molly, I'm sorry. So sorry.

Kenzie curled into a trembling ball, sick with her failure, outraged at the poacher's success. The vultures had come for Molly—what was left of her. Their mission? To clean up Kenzie's latest mess.

"Daddy, Scruffy, Molly. I lost you all. I'm totally worthless." Sobbing, she glanced up at the big birds. "Come on down. Do your job." Then she hid her face and chanted for comfort. "Vultures won't touch me. Vultures won't touch me."

Something crunched through the underbrush.

"Vultures won't touch me. Vultures won't—"

"They might. If you lay there groaning until you die."

Angelo? Kenzie squinted into the sun.

"Come on. Get up, Kenzie. You can't do anything to help this one."

It *was* Angelo. Here. Oh God. She was blubbering like an idiot again. *Stop crying.*

"It's Molly. I can't stand it."

She swallowed.

"I screwed up again."

She sniffed.

"I let Molly get away. Like Scruffy. Now she's dead too."

She sobbed and buried her face in her arms. "I can't do anything right. I mess up over and over. No wonder Dad left." She wiped her nose on her hand, her sleeve, her shirttail. "I don't care if I stay here until I rot."

"Hey, you don't mean that." Angelo handed her his bandana. "Here. Come on. Get up." He helped Kenzie to her feet. "Talk to me. Who's Molly?"

She pointed over her shoulder. "The little deer we saved. I didn't find her in time. Now look at her."

Angelo squinted, wrinkling his forehead, as

though both what he saw and thought hurt. He grew so still and quiet it was a wonder a vulture didn't swoop down and land on his shoulder.

"How can you be so calm? What's wrong with you? You're not the least bit upset about this, this—"

"Kenzie—" He took the bandana, then stuffed it back in his pocket. "This isn't that little doe. Trust me. It's a buck."

"A buck?" Kenzie sniffed.

"Yeah. It has nubby antlers."

"It's not Molly?"

"No way."

"Wow. That's a relief. I mean, it's still crappy, cruddy awful."

"No ship."

"What'd you say?"

"Just agreeing, nautically speaking. Come on. Let's get out of here."

"Was it shot?"

"Trapped, from the looks of its leg. It was field dressed. Butchered for its meat." Angelo nudged Kenzie forward. "So, why'd you think it was the little doe? Didn't the refuge people pick her up?"

"They couldn't."

"How come?"

"Because—" She chewed her ponytail. No way to deny reality.

"Because why?"

"Because they don't know where she is."

"You didn't call them?"

"We couldn't."

"Sure you don't mean, *you wouldn't*?" He stepped in front of her. "You're not still thinking you can keep her?"

"Couldn't if I tried."

"What are you not telling me?"

"I don't know where she is. When I got up she was gone, and the gate was open."

"That sucks." Angelo took her hand.

Her *snotty* hand.

"Let's get out of here." He led her further from the buzzards. "Were you looking for her in those woods?"

"Yes. Exactly." She pulled her hand out of his. "See that opening across the field? I came out there. I've been looking for Molly all morning. The buzzards terrified me. But I figured out what they were. Then I followed them and found the... mess."

He looked up at the buzzards still soaring, waiting their turn.

She wiped her hand on her shorts. "Why

would someone butcher a deer and leave the remains? It's disgusting enough to kill a deer, but to leave it out where anyone could stumble across it—" She wiggled her fingers. *Hey, the hand. It's clean now.* But his attention was focused elsewhere

"It wasn't supposed to be found. A poacher wouldn't leave evidence in plain sight. I think we spooked the killer before he finished taking all the meat. Some's missing, but some's untouched."

"This place gets worse and worse." Kenzie's eyes threatened to pour again.

"This particular place *is* gruesome. Looks like it's the creep's personal butcher shop." He gazed at the opposite edge of the field. "The buzzards started on a pile of remains over there. Your find was a bonus."

"Oh, God." Kenzie hugged her stomach. "He could still be here. He could come after us."

"He won't. He's gone."

"How do you know?"

"Just do." Angelo hooked his thumbs in his pockets. "So, I saw the vultures circling, tied up my boat, and checked it out. Didn't expect to hear you. Pretty impressive battle cry."

Was he smirking?

"Hard to miss your screeching attack on the

vulture air force. At least you managed to scare the killer away." He saluted the patient giants still poised in the distant trees. "Those guys seemed to enjoy the show."

She scowled at him. "Bee boogers."

"What'd you say?"

"Bee boogers. Just kidding, nasally speaking."

He knuckle-bumped her shoulder. "You know, you're okay, for a chick."

"Thanks, I think. Like I said, what makes you so sure the killer's gone?"

Angelo pulled a fishing weight out of his pocket. He rolled it round and round like a ball of clay between his palms. "I think the killer had plenty of time to get to the canal before we found the deer."

He closed the weight in one fist, then smacked it into his other palm like a baseball in a mitt. "While you were busy barfing, Jigs' red runabout flew out of the canal like a wahoo peeling line. I thought he'd shaded something in the stern with his tarp. But I was wrong."

Angelo hurled the weight to the ground. "Not shaded. Hidden."

Chapter 6

Angelo bent down to retrieve the weight. He hesitated, grimacing at Kenzie as he pocketed it.

What, had she sprouted warts?

"Wow, you better get out of this sun. Your freckles will melt together." He headed toward the tree line along the canal. "Come on. I'll take you back in my boat."

Kenzie caught up to him and poked him in the back. "Hey, I hate freckle jokes. I've had to deal with them my whole life. I'm sick of them."

"Sorry, didn't know you were so touchy." Angelo beamed at her over his shoulder. "They're pretty spectacular, though."

She chewed her lip and studied Angelo from behind. He had to have some trait she could pick on. *Skinny? Nah.* Skinny was good. Easier to watch his muscles work. *Eyes? Nope.* Kind of mesmerizing, when they were calm. *Hair? Nice.* Thick and wavy, best she could tell from what extended below his ball cap and hugged his ears. *Ears!* That was it. She caught up with him.

"Hey. Wondered if you were still back there. You sure are quiet. You really are touchy, aren't you?"

"Isn't everyone? About something?" Kenzie transformed herself into Scarlett O'Hara, all syrupy venom. "Surely you're sensitive about something. Aren't you touchy about your ears? I can understand how you would be. I would never comment on them, though. I think it's wonderful how they prop up your hat so it doesn't slide down and blind you."

He flicked a sideways look at her, like maybe she had sunstroke, but he didn't want to say so and scare her.

Kenzie rolled on. "How extraordinary to have ears that can keep hair out of your face. I wish I were so lucky. Why, I need all manner of silly things to restrain mine behind my dainty little ears."

"Are you crazy?" Angelo stopped to cup his fingers around his ears.

Kenzie giggled, relieving waves of tension.

"I'm teasing. Okay?"

His eyes narrowed. "Got it. Snaggin' my line. Fine, but I still think you're nuts. My boat's over there."

"Don't you drive? A car, I mean."

"Not very often. We only have Dad's truck."

"Bummer."

"Not really. Driving's limited. The only road is U.S. 1 for a hundred miles, except for side roads that dead end at the water. That's where my freedom starts. Give me a boat any day."

Wow. Kenzie stopped. He was so different from kids back home. They lived to get their licenses. Truth was they didn't drive much either. City traffic was rough, and subways much faster.

"You having a flashback or something?"

"No. Thinking. Shouldn't we do something about the deer? Like maybe go back and bury it?"

"No, I'll call the refuge. The wildlife officers need to see it."

Good. She didn't want to see that horror again.

As they scrambled down the bank, leggy

mangrove roots provided firm handholds. Angelo climbed on board, rocking the little white boat gently. Kenzie followed and lowered herself onto the bow seat.

Angelo tested the outboard. "We're good to go. Untie the line."

Kenzie freed the rope from a protruding, sharp-angled root, then dropped it into the boat. "When I ran through the tangled trees yesterday to save the dog—*deer*"—she caught his fleeting smirk—"I tripped over one of these weird roots. That's why I fell in. It's nice to know they're good for something."

"Real good in storms. We tie our boats off in mangrove stands. They're tough-stubborn. Dad says they remind him of me. Calls them Angel trees."

"I don't get it. What's the connection?"

Angelo pushed off with a paddle and putt-putted down the canal.

Was he ignoring her?

Finally, he allowed his answer to leak out of the corner of his mouth. "Angel's my real name."

Of course, Ángel. In Spanish *Ángel* sounds sort of like *an hil*. His dad wasn't yelling about anthills last night. He was calling to Angelo.

Kenzie spun on the seat to face him. "So how come you go by Angelo?"

"The guys pinned it on me when we were kids. I'm a pizza freak. Like that makes me Italian." He waved his hand in circles, pretending to spin pizza dough. "It hung on like mangroves to shores." He gassed the engine and spoke above the outboard's surging *glub*. "You know, lots of fish live in mangrove trees."

"In trees?" She couldn't help herself. "Flying fish, right?"

Angelo flashed his you're-nuts look again. "They live in the shallows around the roots. The juvies—barracuda, snapper. Actually, there are flying fish, but they don't really—"

"Angelo, c'mon!"

"Right." He mumbled, "Snaggin' again."

Kenzie peered into the water's black depth, grateful to be on the canal rather than in it. "You hungry?"

"Starving. I thought I'd be home by now."

"Me too. We can get something at my house."

She dangled her fingers in the water. Jerked them out as the boat skimmed through floating seaweed. "Ew. I bet that's the scratchy stuff you dragged me through yesterday."

"Yep."

"I must be allergic to it. My face and arms itch."

"Nobody's allergic to that stuff."

He switched to idle, then reached for her hand.

An unfamiliar feeling shimmied up her spine. *Relief, right?* He'd taken the hand she trailed in the water. Snot-free.

Angelo inspected her arm. He leaned forward and peered at her face. She closed her eyes. Thick, slow heat flowed up her neck like hot lava and flushed her cheeks.

"You're breaking out in red blotches."

She opened her eyes. *Ohmigod.* He was right. Major mortification.

"Hate to tell you, the stuff you ran into doesn't cause rashes. But it's a problem when it decays. Smells like rotten eggs."

"Well, somebody should spray weed killer on that seaweed."

"Poison the water?" Angelo dropped Kenzie's hand like her freckles had pounced on his arm. "You *are* nuts! Better hope the Marine Patrol never hears you say that. And it's not a weed, it's seagrass. Turtle grass to be exact."

She'd done it again. Gone stupid. Weren't

ugly blotches embarrassing enough? Which wicked chick possessed her this time, Kelly Klutz or Debbie Ditz? Whenever Angelo was around, one of them snatched her brain. *Deflect the ditz, Kenzie. Snag away.*

She poured on the big tease. "How interesting. Floating seaweed called turtle grass? I suppose if you saw a pile of grass out in the ocean, from a distance it might look like a turtle."

"Unbelievable." He grimaced like she'd called a turtle a shark. "It's called turtle grass because..." He maneuvered the little boat around a downed buttonwood tree. "It's like dog chow. Get it?"

He was the one who didn't get it.

"Think. Chow for dogs—dog chow. Grass for turtles—turtle grass. Sea turtles are herbivores."

Did he honestly think she was that dumb? Hours of observing glacial-size tanks at the New York Aquarium, its mystical echo and comforting pungent odor, plus weeks of science project research reeled in Kenzie's mind. But she would quietly reel him in. How long before he caught on and spit out the bait? This was going to be fun.

"Oh, I have so much to learn about this exotic

locale." Wide-eyed, Kenzie fluffed the hair off her neck. "I never would have imagined that sea turtles don't eat fish. Are you sure that's true of all sea turtles?"

"That's what I said, isn't it?"

She rubbed her cheeks as if his words had spattered them. He was taking this way too seriously.

Pausing dramatically between each harsh word, Angelo launched them one by one. "Herbivore—means—plant—eater, not—meat—eater."

Kenzie scratched her neck.

"You should have learned that in your big city school."

She scratched her arms.

"Listen carefully: *herb-i-vore*. Now you try saying it."

She'd totally snagged his line. He was way too tight, not giving her a fraction of slack. Her escalating itch factor and his *you-try-saying-it* comment had ripped all play out of her too. She scratched and snapped, "How about I say *carn-i-vore* instead. That's what you're acting like—a nasty, carnivorous shark. You, an angel? Ha!"

Angelo approached the dock wearing a face that could have been carved on Mt. Rushmore.

Stone silent, he cut the engine and tossed the rubber bumpers over the side. The boat glided until it knocked against the concrete.

Kenzie's encyclopedic knowledge of sea turtles was about to explode. If she opened her mouth now, her words would torch him like dragon fire. She had to get out of the boat. Find proof. Show him. She jumped onto the dock before Angelo tied the lines. "Okay, Sharkman. Upstairs. Sandwiches in the fridge."

She flew up the back step and beelined to her room. Where was that science book? The box in the closet. She dug for a green-and-yellow cover. Found it. She glanced through the index, then found the section on sea turtles.

Okay, Sharkman. Let me fill you in. Wait. Even better. She hadn't cleaned out her school stuff yet. She tilted the threadbare bag and mined through the mess of papers, hair clips, pencils, pens, CDs, snack wrappers, and old tissues.

Bingo. She struck gold. No. She giggled. Not gold, pink. She pulled out the highlighter. Skimming sentences, she swiped the choicest with bold pink stripes.

First she highlighted, *Leatherbacks are carnivorous and feed primarily on jellyfish.* Next, she pinked, *Hawksbills are omnivorous and feed on algae, grass, fish, and sponges.* Third, *The loggerhead turtle,* Caretta caretta (she included the Latin for its poetic flair), *crushes crustaceans and mollusks and also feeds on jellyfish and sponges.* Oh, how the evidence built. Finally, she highlighted, *For the first year of their life, green turtles are carnivorous; after one year they are herbivorous.*

She marched into the kitchen and presented the pinkened page to Angelo. "Okay, Sharkman, can you r-e-a-d, read?"

Angelo sat at the counter. His eyes darted over the page from pink line to pink line. When he put the book down, he tilted his head and shrugged. "Your point would be?" He grinned like a toddler caught stealing a cookie.

"My point would be that I learned the correct stuff in New York. I'm not stupid, and I wish you'd learn when I'm teasing."

"Okay, okay. I give. You're one up." He held up a finger. "So, stick with me here: green—grass—weeds. Can we agree that it's the *green* sea turtle that looks most like a pile of floating sea*grass,* an ocean plant that many otherwise intelligent people call sea*weed?*"

Amazing. How easily he'd flushed away her anger. She stared at him a few seconds before

55

she let the giggles escape. Maybe he wasn't a total shark after all. She could have hugged him. Instead she swatted his arm and pulled a bag of potato chips out of the cabinet.

"You know," Angelo said, "Dad tells me I need to stop and think before I speak."

She wished his dad would talk with the Klutz and Ditz chicks.

"Maybe my dad's right. Do we have a truce?"

"Truce. Let's eat." She sat on the other side of the counter. They opened the zippered plastic bags and dug into the sandwiches.

"Why were you over here today? Fishing the canal?"

"Not the canal, the channel. There wasn't much action," he explained between bites. "I got to wondering how you'd contact the refuge. I didn't know if your phone was hooked up or if you had a cell. So I came up the canal to find out if you needed mine."

"I don't have one. I swamped it at my last swim meet, and our landline isn't working yet. Turns out it didn't much matter, though."

"Yeah. Got to do something about that. I'll find her."

His jaw twitched as he spoke. *Nerves or*

anger? Hard to tell.

"Anyway, when I noticed the buzzards landing, I got curious. The rest is history."

"Listen, if Mom finds out I left the house, she'll sentence me to one of her famous *you'll-be-lucky-to-get-out-of-here-before-you-can-vote* groundings." She pointed her sandwich at him. "Don't mention one word about this morning around her, ever."

"No problem." He pushed back his stool. "It'll be out of my head before I'm out of the canal. I need to get home."

"Wait." Kenzie hurried to the bathroom. She ripped the packing tape off a box labeled *First Aid*. The cortisone tube was in plain sight. Minutes later she rushed into the kitchen, white streaks lining her face and arms like war paint. "I don't believe you. You're not going home. You're going after Jigs, and I'm going with you."

Chapter 7

"NO WAY. I'm not taking you with me. Not with that rash. It's ninety-five degrees out. Think about it. What'd you say about getting grounded?"

"I said I'd be grounded if Mom finds out. Simple. We get home before she does."

"*We* aren't going."

"Look, I want to know what Jigs hid in his boat as much as you do. Maybe more. Besides, you might need help."

"Help? From you?" He tossed his balled-up napkin into a box full of trash. "Planning another blitz? This time by sea? Shi...p, Kenzie. You blast in like a storm trooper, I'll never find anything."

Kenzie smoldered. She swigged her soda to cool her tongue. But her eyes flamed. "I'm—

not—stupid. Remember?"

"Sorry." Angelo waved the peace sign and lowered his volume. "But I'm dead serious. I'm not taking you with me. Got it?"

"I got it. I don't like it though."

"Sorry, Red. I need to do this on my own."

"But I could— Hey, what's with *Red*?"

"Uh. It's a Keys thing. You need a handle. You know, like mine. Italian pizza guy, Angelo."

Sharkman was more like it. "Why *Red*? My freckles or hair?"

He munched some potato chips. "Neither. This morning, the way you blazed after those buzzards. You were intense. Roared through that field like wildfire."

Yeah, right. Impressive, though. Hard not to admire a good save when you hear one.

Angelo patted his pocket. "Anyway, I've got my phone. Before I take off, call the refuge about your doe. So what if we don't know where she is. Tell them number 77's out there injured somewhere. The volunteers and staff can be on the lookout for her."

"Why me? You're calling them about the dead deer. You tell them."

"Nope, 77—Molly—is your story. They should know how you saved her. It's a great story."

"It kind of is, isn't it?"

"Bet your Dad loved it."

Kenzie smirked. "I don't think it made the news in New York."

"So call him too. I have unlimited minutes." He slid his tiny phone across the counter to her.

Kenzie recoiled as if he'd released a tarantula. "Not going to happen. I don't talk to him. Not in person, not on the computer, and not on the phone."

Questions furrowed Angelo's brow. He shook them off as if to cut the dad subject loose. "Got a phonebook?"

Kenzie rifled through Nana's kitchen drawers, slamming one after the other closed until she found a tattered phone book. She abused its already crumpled pages in her search. "Here's the number." She swiveled the book to show him.

He folded his arms. "Your story, remember?"

Kenzie slumped on the stool and smashed phone keys like they were offensive ants.

The answering refuge officer's compassionate nature and warm voice soothed Kenzie. As she summarized events for him, Kenzie doused angry sparks one by one until, while describing her mother's successful CPR, she actually smiled. At the end of her story, she explained, "But last night Molly disappeared," and one last ember threatened. Crap, her voice was cracking. *Do not cry, Kenzie.*

His collar question focused her. "Yes, sir. There was a tag. Number 77." Kenzie shot out of her seat. "No way! She's safe? I don't believe it."

She covered the receiver. "Angelo, something wonderfully weird happened."

"He knows something about the deer?"

She signaled *give me a minute.*

"But, officer, she was limping." Kenzie paced tight circles around the kitchen. "How could she make it over there? She couldn't put herself into a pen. Are you sure the tag is number 77? Sorry, that was a silly question."

Officer Kaczynski suggested she come see for herself.

"You mean it? Wow, thanks. Watson Boulevard, right? Yes. I'm on my way."

She hung up and handed Angelo his phone.

"Hey, you hung up before I told him about the dead deer."

"Call him back. I'm out of here. Molly's at the Refuge Maintenance Center.It's incredible. I won't believe it until I see her. How do I get to the end of Watson Boulevard? Is it too far to ride my bike?" She rushed out the back door and down the steps before he opened his mouth.

"Hey!" Angelo raced after her.

Her words kept time with her feet. "The officer said I can go see her. He'll meet me there. He seems nice. He knows I want to be sure it's Molly. Isn't it amazing?"

"Red, you're all fired up again. Slow down. I can figure out how to get you there in my boat. Give me time to check the chart."

Kenzie gripped the handlebars of her bike. "They don't have a clue how she got there. The officer said when he arrived at the Maintenance Center this morning, Molly was sleeping in the pen with the gate closed." She flipped up the kickstand.

"Hey, I said I'd get you there in the boat."

"Just tell me where it is."

"It's a long bike ride, Kenzie. If you won't let me take you, wait until your mom can."

"I'm not waiting. I have to see Molly now. I have to know that she's okay. Don't you get it? I have to make sure."

"And Dad thinks I'm stubborn."

Kenzie pushed her bike out from under the house. Angelo trailed behind spitting out street directions and heat warnings. When she reached the road, she stopped and straddled the seat.

Angelo kicked pea rock at the rear wheel. Pebbles scattered around her feet.

Kenzie shot him a look. "That's mature."

"Who cares if you get heat stroke? Get out of here." Angelo smacked the bike's fender. "Better for me anyway. I'll find Jigs quicker if I don't have to haul you around first."

"If you do find him, don't bite his head off before you learn something, Sharkman." Kenzie hopped on the seat and pedaled off.

Angelo yelled after her. "You'll never make it home before your mom does."

Chapter 8

SIT IN A BOAT? *Wait for Mom? Impossible.* Kenzie had to do something.

Heart pounding, legs pumping, she propelled her bike with ninth-inning intensity. A runner screaming home in a tie game. Pedal, pump. Pedal, pump. Round and round. The circular rhythm unwound her, made way for brain function. She needed a plan. Her mom expected unpacking progress.

Twenty minutes later she turned onto the bike path along Key Deer Boulevard, weird title for a road with light traffic and a 35-mph speed limit. She'd figured out what to do. As soon as she got home, she'd empty a few big boxes, spread stuff around, then unpack the computer and hook it up. She had lots of brand-new-in-the-box software. Smarmy bribes from her dad. Toss software packaging around, and her mom would assume the usual installation issues had eaten up Kenzie's time.

Kenzie flapped her elbows, airing her sticky underarms. She'd expected bike riding to be easy because the island was flat. It was. Flat brutal under a tropical sun. Especially here where the endless path took her through a scorched wasteland of naked sticks. Sticks that stabbed a mockingly blue sky. Drops of perspiration salted her eyes, rolled down her back. She slumped on the handlebars, sinking into the oatmeal-thick air.

Her bike rebelled. With a mechanical mind of its own, it wandered randomly over the path. Pavement and plants blurred, levitated, transformed into mysterious images. She'd left the planet, abducted by aliens experimenting on Earthlings' tolerance for global warming. She was a panting, gasping, human rat.

Kenzie slogged on. Airways clogged. Lungs congested. Were the aliens pumping the atmosphere with twice as many H atoms as O? *Water, water killing me, but not a drop to drink.*

Splat. A palm branch smacked Kenzie's head. She raised a hand to fend off her attacker. The green palm frond waved at her. Earth to Kenzie. Wait. Palm frond? She blinked. She'd made it to a forest of healthy palms and lush vegetation, left desolation behind.

She pushed on, but the intermittent shade didn't relieve her parched exhaustion. The cortisone wasn't working either. She let go of the right handlebar to scratch her face. *Yikes!* A brown flash shot out of the trees in front of her. Deer! She jerked the handlebars. Lost control. *Bam.* Slammed the ground. Slid across the hot blacktop. *Crap. Crap. Cra-a-ap!* But no blaring horns. No screeching tires. She opened her eyes. Not a car in sight. Deer either. A balanced bag of luck.

She flexed her bloody knees. No problem. Bent her skinned elbows. Sore, but functioning. Examined her grit-encrusted palms and wiggled her fingers. Everything was working. Except her plan. She righted the bike and stood, surveyed the damage. That busy-putting-together-the-computer excuse wasn't going to fly with these road burns; technology fights had never left her bloody. She'd figure something else out. Later. Right now, she had to concentrate on getting to Molly.

Kenzie finally reached Watson Boulevard, another narrow road with a big name. Aching and itching, she turned west and wobbled to the top of a narrow bridge. She squinted into the sun

and groaned. Another bridge glared at her. She reached the top and collapsed on the seat. The bike picked up downhill speed, and Kenzie lifted her face to greet the rush of air. There it was: the end of the road. Her eyes teared as she rolled past the open gates to the Refuge Maintenance Center.

Both sides of the narrow entrance road were lined with mangroves. Through the thick "Angel trees" she glimpsed sparkles of turquoise water. A dark bronze plaque on a coral rock assured her she was in the right place, *Key Deer National Wildlife Refuge, Established 1954.* Kenzie turned into the driveway and parked at an open garage door beside a pickup truck emblazoned with a Florida Fish and Wildlife Service insignia.

"Who could this be but our heroine, Kenzie Ryan?"

Sunblind, Kenzie turned toward the deep velvety voice.

A shadow emerged from the garage. "It's a pleasure to meet you, young lady."

The officer wore dark brown shorts, a tan shirt. Her eyes adjusted, and she read his brass nameplate—*Mike Kaczynski.* Kenzie struggled to speak. "Nice to meet—" Deep breath. "You too—" Another breath. "Officer Kaczynski." Two more huffs. "Where—is Molly? How—is she?"

"In the pen out back. She's fine, but you don't look so good. Let's get you out of the sun. You need some fluids."

"I'm okay." She wiped her forehead on her sleeve. "Just hot and tired."

"Please, Kenzie, come inside." The officer's soothing voice came from a dreamy distance. Blazing lights exploded behind her eyes. "Careful there, young lady." His face whirled and his words echoed. "Careful there, young lady. Careful there, young lady."

She floated for ages, soared with great kite-like birds, and drifted into a peaceful, dark cave until a cool touch on her face and neck roused her. "Wow, that feels good." Nearby a fan droned, and a breeze flowed over her. "What happened?"

A gentle hand raised her head. "You're dehydrated. Sip a little of this. Your pretty freckled face is one red beet. You're looking very wilted."

Kenzie mumbled, "My freckles are not melted."

Officer Kaczynski laughed as if he were watching a puppy chase butterflies.

Kenzie supported her weight on her forearms until she was steady. Then she sat and swung her legs over the side of the little cot. "I'm fine. Honest. I'm sorry I caused you trouble. But I'm okay now. Let's go see Molly."

"You're no trouble, Kenzie, and, yes, I know you'll be fine. You exerted yourself too much in this heat. Here, couple more sips. Didn't you tell me on the phone that you moved here from somewhere up north?"

She nodded and sipped. "Thanks. Can we—"

"You need time to adjust to our climate. Things are a little different down here."

No ship, as Angelo would say. This place would kill her yet, if her mom or Angelo didn't do it first.

"You need a hat and sunglasses." He held out the cup. "Another one. Did you wear sunscreen?"

Kenzie swallowed. "No." She set the cup on a little table and then pushed up from the cot.

"Not yet." Mike rested a hand on her arm. Her heart calmed and her breathing eased, as if his hand had drawn the tension out of her body. Totally weird.

He urged her to drink more. "Always carry water with you."

How out of it was she exactly? This guy

sounded like Mom in disguise. Every word could have come straight out of Mom's mouth. *Mom.* Yikes! If Kenzie didn't get home fast, her mother would freak.

"Officer Kaczynski, please, I want to see Molly."

"Call me Mike. I'm beginning to think that red face of yours is more than heat exhaustion. Look at your arms."

She stretched out her arms and turned them over.

Mike gestured to a number of angry blotches. "Looks like a rash of some kind."

"Maybe I got sunburned. You know, since I didn't put on sunscreen."

She waited for more Mom talk like, *Don't you ever stop to think?*

Instead he said, "Okay, get up slowly. Go wash your hands and knees." He indicated the bathroom. "Then we'll visit your friend. I'll wait for you outside."

Kenzie found Mike organizing equipment in the back of his truck. He closed the tailgate, then led her to a little peninsula that jutted into a bay where three boats rocked on anchors. As they approached a chain-link pen, Mike said, "There's your mystery girl."

Molly dozed under a shed in the far corner. Kenzie hooked her fingers into the links. "Hi, Molly. Remember me? I worried about you all night, and most of today, until I found out where you were. I sure wish you could tell us how you got here. Come say *hello*. That's it. Hey, you're not limping one little bit."

Molly stopped to scratch her ears with a rear hoof. Kenzie's arms begged for similar attention. She curled her fingers into fists and, trying not to scratch, rubbed her rash.

"You know," Mike said, "I think she may have only seemed hurt because she was sore and a little hesitant to put weight on her legs. She'll be fit and strong before you know it."

Rubbing offered pitiful itch relief. Kenzie gave up and scratched.

"I'm more concerned about you. When did that itching start?"

"Yesterday. At first I thought it was from the turtle grass in the canal, but Angelo told me that wouldn't make me itch."

"He's right. By the way, before you arrived someone who called himself Angelo phoned me about your sad discovery. He helped you rescue this deer, right?"

She nodded.

"I assume his given name is *Ángel*. Or as we'd say, Angel. Angel Sanchez. It's nice to know he and his dad are still here. I haven't seen them since Mrs. Sanchez died this spring."

Angelo's mom? Dead? Her throat burned, and her stomach knotted. No. Couldn't be. He'd never said a word.

Mike studied her face. "This rash came on after your swim in the canal, huh? Well, it can't be the grass, and there have been no reports of sea lice in the canals—"

"Sea lice?" Kenzie squealed.

"Well, sea nettles may be a more appropriate name. Though, it could have been a larger jellyfish that stung you. Hmmm."

"Lice? Nettles? Jellyfish? Are you serious?"

"Don't worry. I don't think any of those critters got you. You said you were looking for the deer in the hammock, right?"

Rudolph lounging in a striped canvas swing? He was kidding, right? "I was looking in the *woods*."

"Exactly." Mike smiled. Something he did frequently, judging from the white valleys in his tanned skin. "Mystery solved. You have poisonwood."

Deer killers, stinky seaweed, broiling sun,

heat exhaustion, stinging sea whatevers, and now poisonwood. She crossed her arms and dug into her skin, up and down, back and forth.

"I want to go home." But she couldn't return to the home she meant. If she didn't let off steam she'd explode. *Move, Kenzie.*

"Mike, I have to go." *Now.*

"Wait." Mike put a hand on her shoulder. Again the tension flowed right out of her. He was a giant stress sponge.

"No more sun for you today. I'll take you home. We'll throw your bike in the back of the truck. First, let's go to the medical room, and we'll put some cortisone cream on that rash."

"I did that. It didn't help."

"Your sweat could have washed it off, and exertion makes it itch worse. I recommend you see a doctor for a shot."

"Mom's a nurse. She'll know what to do." But how would Kenzie explain catching poisonwood?

"That's right. She administered CPR to the deer. Some lady. I'd like to meet her."

The medical room was fascinating. Its ceiling-high shelves were full of supplies: antiseptic, plastic gloves, rolls of cotton, needles, alcohol, even a stethoscope. There were charts and files and boards covered with mounted jawbones and teeth that indicated the age and diet of the deceased.

"I feel like I'm in a science lab or an emergency room," Kenzie said.

"More like an emergency room. People call us at all hours of the night and day to report injured or sick deer. We pick them up and bring them here for a checkup. Here's our people kit." He took out a tube of cream. "This will help that itch."

"It's obvious how deer get injured—*too obvious*—but what makes them sick?"

"All deer are susceptible to stomach worms. Bucks can contract a dizzying brain disease, and now and then one will get a rare case of tuberculosis. In fact, considering how your mother administered CPR to a deer, she should get tested to be sure she hasn't picked that up."

"What? Mom could have TB?"

He squeezed cream on his gloved finger, then patted it on her arm. "Easy. I'm sure she doesn't, but it's simple for her to be tested, and it's the safe thing to do." He handed the tube to her. "You finish the job."

Mike trashed his gloves, then put the kit away on a shelf beside a display board that read, *Samples of Items Found in Key Deer Stomachs.* Attached to the board were plastic flowers, strands of wire, balloons, Easter basket grass, fishing line, and rope. Apparently, deer swallowed horrible junk while rummaging in garbage cans. "Mike, how often—"

"Excuse me." He checked his cell phone. "I'll be right back." Mike went into his office for a few minutes, then returned looking grim. "There's an emergency, but I can take you home first."

"Is it a deer?"

He started toward the truck. "Come on. I want to tell you about an interesting Web site you might enjoy."

Nice try. "It *is* a deer, isn't it? Was another one killed?"

"I don't know yet. We'd better get a move on. Your mother will be worried about you." He glanced at his watch. "It's after four o'clock."

No way. Kenzie raced to the truck. Grounded for life.

Chapter 9

Mike clicked off the ignition.

Kenzie's mom charged down the steps—both barrels loaded—one with panic, the other with anger.

Kenzie practiced rabbit freeze.

"Where have you been?" Her mom stared at the truck and shrieked, "What have you done? Are you under arrest?"

Before Mike closed the truck door, he switched to emergency management mode. "Ms. Ryan—wonderful!" He crossed in front of the truck to greet her. "You *are* home. How lucky."

Lucky?

"It's a pleasure to meet you." He extended his hand. "Mike Kaczynski, your friendly fish and wildlife officer."

Kenzie's mom fluffed her hair and got all wiggly-wide-eyed.

This situation wasn't lucky. It was yucky.

"Please"—if her mom were a cat, she'd have purred—"Call me Maggie."

Maggie? Where'd that come from?

Mike lifted Kenzie's bike out of the truck bed and shot her a now-would-be-a-good-time-to-move-your-butt look.

Kenzie slipped out of the truck and eased the passenger door shut.

He leaned the bike against the porch steps. "I was pleased that your daughter responded when I asked her to come identify the deer."

Asked her to come? This guy was slick.

"Then, when I learned how you performed CPR on the deer, I was eager to meet you. Your daughter takes after you. She's a brave and responsible young lady."

Her mom's eyebrows twitched up in surprise, then lowered under weighty forehead wrinkles, as if focusing on the image of Kenzie as a responsible young lady was a struggle.

Kenzie bit back her grin.

"Ms. Ry— Sorry, Maggie, you must be very proud of your daughter."

Her mom's eyes drifted to Kenzie. "Yes, I

must be," she said, as if she'd packed that pride, but couldn't remember where. Then she focused and stepped closer to Kenzie. "Honey, what did you do to your face?"

Uh-oh.

"And arms? And knees?" Her mom's voice rose with each question.

Was Mad Mother Margaret about to show after all?

"A deer ran in front of my bike. I crashed and—"

"And with so much poisonwood on refuge land," Mike said, "I'm certain she got into it. That's what's breaking out on her arms and face. This heat aggravated it."

"Poor baby." Nurse Mom lifted Kenzie's face to study the rash. "Your skin is so sensitive." She turned up Kenzie's palms. "And look at your hands. Your knees. You're a mess. What am I going to do with you?" She stepped back, held her forehead, and searched the sky for an answer.

"Well, ladies, I have business to attend to. Maggie—" He touched her mom's elbow.

Her mother snapped to attention and extended an arm to shake hands. Mike held her hand a moment while her face smoothed and her shoulders relaxed.

"Thank you, Mike," she said softly. "Thank you for driving Kenzie home."

Kenzie dozed and drifted, merging and sorting thoughts and images as the morning light peeked around her shades. Had Angelo found Jigs? Angelo's theory made sense. Jigs must have hidden deer meat in his boat. The trap too.

Could Mike's emergency have involved Jigs? Maybe he'd been arrested. A happy end to the poaching. No. Mike had not looked happy after that call.

He had saved her big time though. Mom felt sorry for her. No complaints about unpacked boxes, no lectures about taking off without permission, and no questions about the origin of poisonwood. She'd lathered on cortisone cream, said she'd take Kenzie for a shot in the morning, and that was it.

"Kenzie, are you up?"

Kenzie blinked away lingering images.

"The clinic closes at ten on Saturdays. And I want to make it to the flea market before it's too hot and crowded. Shake a leg."

"Okay." Kenzie groaned and made a behind-closed-doors face. Flea markets. Bunches of old junk. She'd been lucky yesterday, so she'd better humor Mom today. "I'll be out in a minute."

It was prime grazing time when Kenzie and her mom left for town. Deer seemed to be everywhere munching grass in yards, devouring flowers and shrubs, and nibbling foliage along the road.

"We're not even out of the neighborhood, and I've counted thirteen deer," Kenzie said. "It's hard to believe they're endangered when they're all over the place."

"Only all over this tiny spot on Earth, sweetie, which is why I'm baffled that anyone tries to garden here. It's a unique experience living among animals that should be wild, but behave like undisciplined pets."

"True, but they're cute."

"Absolutely, but problematic too. A patient told me one morning when her screen door was open, a deer traipsed in and ate the scrambled eggs off her plate. Eggs. Who'd have thought it?"

"They're wild about potato chips too." Crap. Why'd she mention that?

"Really? So even deer like junk food. How'd you—"

"Angelo. But talking about junk food, Mike told me they eat out of garbage cans. That's serious junk food."

"Sounds dangerous."

"Deadly sometimes. Look, Mom."

They'd turned onto Key Deer Boulevard by an open field where a herd of deer foraged.

"No matter their diet, they seem to be prolific."

Phew. Mom had dropped the potato chip issue. "Yeah, how do they manage that? There are four does, three fawns, and not a buck in sight."

Her mom laughed.

Kenzie sighed. *Absent dads...*

A delay at the clinic meant few shady parking spots were left in the wooded lot when they reached the flea market. In her rush to claim the last, her mom almost ran over a bicycle—one of many left lying on the ground or leaning against a tree. Few were locked. The light-footed New York bike thieves could make a killing down here.

Colorful banners lined the aisles of the flea market advertising toys, artwork, housewares, plants, clothes, and books. It was more than just a lot of old junk. It was a lot of new junk too.

"Honey, can you find someplace to stay out of the sun while I shop for vegetables?"

"No problem. There's a book booth. I'll check it out."

"Super. Try not to scratch that rash or your injection site. Let's meet at the gate in about forty-five minutes."

The book booth was a large gray tent that sheltered ten cafeteria-sized tables. Each was loaded with books stacked in precarious piles in no particular order. The vendor greeted Kenzie with well-rehearsed questions: "What's your interest? Horses? Drawing? Cooking? I've got books on every subject you can imagine, some you can't, and every one's a bargain." Before she could respond, he zeroed in on someone behind her, "Hey, mister. I have the perfect book for you."

The vendor grabbed a copy of *Your Mixed Breed Dog* and hurried out into the sunshine. He thrust it at a tall man who struggled with the leash of a big, shaggy, and very energetic dog. The dark man was lean and solid with the shape of hard work in his muscles—like a sculpture, except for his long gray beard—a living Bronze Man.

The shiny Bronze Man studied the dirt. "No,

sir. I thank you kindly, but that book is of no use to me." With the dog straining at its leash, he turned and walked away.

While Kenzie waited for her mom, Bronze Man waited at the food wagon window. A pinched-faced server snapped at him. "If you'd read first, you would see for yourself what's on the menu. I don't have time to spout off the whole list for you. Obviously, you didn't read that sign over there either." She pointed and spat at him, "The one that says, 'No dogs.'"

"Yes, ma'am." He looked at a child eating a large donut. "I'll just take a donut and water, please, ma'am."

"Seventy-five cents."

He placed a five dollar bill in the woman's hand. She shoved his food and receipt across the counter and threw the change at him as she left the window. He gathered the bills together before the wind could scatter them, but the quarter landed at his feet.

After he counted the change, he called out, "Pardon me, ma'am."

The server returned. "What now?"

"I think you meant this to be a one." Bronze Man returned the five dollar bill to her.

The old witch switched bills and didn't even

thank him.

He pocketed the ones. Then he turned silently and walked away, seeming to carry something much heavier than decades of labor and a donut.

Kenzie was sure he could have used that extra money.

He tied the leash to a post and offered his cup to the thirsty dog. Kenzie had done that same thing for Scruffy so many times.

Melodic whistling pulled Kenzie back to the moment. A small crowd had gathered at a corner of the food pavilion where a comical man sat on a low stool surrounded by homemade instruments. Propped against a tip jar at his feet was a sign identifying him as Whistling Willy. His instruments were fashioned from cans, buckets, spoons, washboards, and other junky things. As he played, he whistled for joy, as if he'd swallowed a mockingbird.

Kenzie sat on a bench, closed her eyes, and bounced to the magical music.

The whistling stopped mid tune, and someone—*Willy?*—said, "Hey, Jigs. How's it goin'?"

Jigs? Kenzie opened her eyes. At the front of the crowd. *Bronze Man.* Whistling Willy saluted him. Could Bronze Man—a man who refused to cheat a crabby server—be Jigs? Could such an honest man be Angelo's criminal? As Bronze Man and his dog headed toward the wooded parking lot, Willy returned to his music.

Bronze Man tossed his cup and papers into the trash barrel by the exit gate. She couldn't let him get away. She had to talk to him. *Yeah, right. And say what?* "Excuse me, but are you Jigs, the guy who's killing deer?" She'd think of something. *Just catch up to him.*

The trash barrel was jammed to the rim. On a pile of discarded newspapers was one paper cup. It had to be his. Something protruded from it. A cash register coupon for two free lunches. She snatched the coupon and followed him toward the parking lot.

"Hey! Whose dog is that?"

Kenzie jumped at the loud words. She'd been deep in formulating a plan. In the maze of parking lot traffic, Bronze Man's dog yapped at the rolling tires of an SUV as if he were chasing a rubber ball. Where was his master?

Oh ship! The dog's leash. It dragged on the ground. It would get caught under the wheels.

Kenzie jammed the coupon in her pocket. She sped off, zigzagging between bikes, trucks, trees, and cars. She had to stop the SUV. Catch the dog. She reached the middle aisle, but the SUV had parked. What happened to the dog?

A horn sounded.

"Git! You stupid mutt!"

There. Two aisles over. The nutty dog attacked a red pickup.

Woof! Woof! He snapped at the wheels. *Woof! Woof! Woof! Snap, snap, snap.*

The driver continued toward the exit, yelling nonstop. The moronic mutt would soon be splattered all over the highway.

Bikes. Unchained. Kenzie leaped on the closest one. Sending frantic I'm-not-a-thief vibes skyward, she sped down a parallel aisle. Could she beat the truck to the exit lane? No. A tie. But what luck. A white VW blocked the exit. The pickup had to stop. The dog stood panting. He looked back and forth—exiting truck, entering car.

Kenzie jumped off the bike. Raced to the dog. *Whomp!* She stomped on the leash. The red pickup went out. The white VW turned in. The dog and Kenzie stood, staring at each other in the middle of traffic.

"I'm no ball. I'm no tire. And I'm not going to play chase, so don't snap at me. Deal?"

The dog's floppy tail rose into the air and wagged in circles.

"Guess it's a deal." Kenzie grabbed the dusty leash and moved out of the exit lane.

"Come with me while I get the bike and return it. And behave. You won't bite its tires will you?" She stretched out her hand, and the goofy dog leaned forward to sniff. "That's it, boy." The dog wiggled all over and jumped up to wash her face. "Hey, down now."

A long shadow appeared next to hers. "Miss, I'll trade you this bike for that very naughty girl." Bronze Man. Pushing the bike she'd borrowed.

Naughty *girl*? Kenzie leaned down and peeked. "Oops! Sorry, girl."

Bronze Man's eyes sparkled and, within that nest of beard, there might have been a grin. "I am much indebted to you, Miss. You are very kind." He steadied the bike, then stooped to ruffle the dog's fur. "Could you not allow me a few private moments without creating a scene?"

Private? The restroom by the exit lane. That's where he'd been.

He rose and held out a weathered, calloused hand. "Jigs and Fisher at your service." He gave a little bow. "We are very pleased to meet you."

The Whistler had said, "Jigs." But was he

talking to the man or the dog? *Who was who?* No matter. Her gut agreed with her brain. This gentle, honest man and his sweet, silly pet couldn't be the poacher and the hunting dog.

Kenzie passed the leash to Bronze Man as he rolled the bike toward her. "I'm happy to meet you too, sir." She pulled the receipt coupon from her pocket. "I think you accidentally dropped this in the trash." She flipped it over. "Bet you don't want to miss two free meals."

"Well now, you are right about that. I must thank you again for your kindness, miss. I did not look at its reverse side." He took the coupon and tugged the leash. "Let's go, pretty girl, before we engage ourselves in additional complications."

Wearing his quiet dignity like a protective cloak, he walked away. The elusive man Angelo planned to hunt down and sneak up on, catch in some criminal act. She'd found him. Found him without trying. Found him innocent. How could she tell Angelo that?

"I met Jigs. (Or Fisher? Best not to mention that possibility yet.) You're wrong, Sharkman. He's noble, kind, and honest. He's not robbing your father's traps or killing deer." And then what? Watch Angelo call her a concrete-brained city chick and walk away in disgust. Forever?

Chapter 10

Kenzie returned the borrowed bike, then headed for the gate between the market and the parking lot. *Uh-oh.* Mom was there already. She'd want to know what Kenzie had been doing in the parking lot. Following a strange man wouldn't cut it. Easier to avoid the question. Changing directions, she entered the market through a side gate.

"Hey, Mom."

"What, no books?"

"Nope." *Switch topics, Kenzie.* "Those are yummy looking tomatoes."

"Aren't they? All these fruits and veggies are super fresh. But I forgot I need to go to the drugstore. Hope they don't cook in the car."

Her mom maneuvered through the parking lot traffic, and Kenzie scanned the grounds for

Bronze Man. No sign of him. Was he driving? Walking? Riding a bike? What direction had he taken? She scanned the roadsides all the way to the shopping center.

"Mom, did you see that? We just passed a sign that keeps count of how many Key deer are killed. Forty-eight so far this year." *How many of those were the sicko poacher's doing? Did he get a thrill every time the count went up?*

"I noticed that sign yesterday. It said forty-six when I saw it."

So, the one Angelo called in made forty-seven. And forty-eight? *Mike's phone call.* Someone *had* found another dead deer. Kenzie closed her eyes. *Stop it.* She visualized racing to home plate to the sound of wild cheering, swimming lazy laps in a clear blue pool, anything but bloody deer remains.

Kenzie waited outside in the shade while her mom shopped. Her poisonwood rash flared and itched with the rising temperature. *Stop thinking. Stop scratching.*

The hot southern wind had picked up, rolling cups in awkward circles, whipping newspapers, fliers, and candy wrappers across the parking lot. Look at that junk. She took off in an awkward dance, chasing and collecting trash. Step. Step. Scoop. She jammed handfuls of litter into the sidewalk trash bin. Step. Step. Scoop.

What turned people into such slobs? Maybe it was accidental. Garbage bags could fall out of a pickup truck bed. Trash could bounce out of a trailered boat. Papers could blow out of an open car door.

Step. Step. Stomp. Kenzie trapped a runaway newspaper page against the curb, reached for it, and froze. The headline screamed, *Severed Deer Head Dumped on Refuge Property*. Each word a sucker punch. Sick. Sick. Sick.

Kenzie stumbled to the Jeep and folded onto the front seat. She sat in a daze, arms wrapped around her knees, until the driver's door opened.

"Kenzie, what's wrong?" Her mom pulled the newspaper from Kenzie's grasp. "Oh, dear Lord." She drew Kenzie close and held her, finger-combing her windblown hair. Then she raised Kenzie's face. "Baby, there's nothing you can do about this. Please, try not to let it bother you so.

At least it wasn't the deer you saved."

Slowly, her mom released Kenzie, then reached into a bag and withdrew a new tube of cortisone. She held the tube, while stroking Kenzie's face with her free hand, as if to wipe away the pain before applying the cream.

Kenzie pushed her mom's hand away. "How do I know it wasn't our little deer? Maybe Mike released her, and the poacher shot her already."

Her mom picked up the paper. "Did you read the whole thing? No, I guess not. It would have just upset you more. Look at this."

Kenzie stared out the window.

"Okay, I'll tell you what it says. It was a six-point buck. It was not your deer."

"What difference does it make? It's still a dead deer." *Another one.* Kenzie's eyes burned. "How can people be so despicable? Throwing garbage all over the place is sick enough, but cutting off a little deer's—" The lump in her stomach ballooned and trapped her words.

"I don't have the answers, baby. I don't think anyone does." Her mom smoothed Kenzie's hair behind her ears and kissed her forehead. "We've just got to concentrate on all the good people out there. There's nothing we can do about the bad ones. Come on. Let's go home."

As they pulled out onto Key Deer Boulevard, Kenzie burst out, "I don't want to believe there's nothing we can do. I'm going to do something. I don't know what yet, but I'm going to do something."

"Right now, you're going to go home and eat. Then, while I unpack more boxes, you can set up your computer. You need to have it ready when the cable company gets here. They're going to come on a Saturday. That would have never happened in New York. Now please stop worrying about things you can't fix."

As they approached the ball field, her mom slowed the Jeep and hunched over the steering wheel. "Look." She stared up through the windshield. "There's a huge osprey nest on the light pole behind home plate. If you played here, you could watch the chicks grow. Hope they don't poop on the fans."

Mom was doing her talk-and-distract thing, but it wouldn't work. Worries kept piling up. *Like intentional deer killings—*

"It will be good to get your computer going, honey."

And Angelo blaming the wrong man—

"You'll be able to keep up with your friends back in New York."

And jerks dumping garbage all over the island—

"Your father is going to call you this afternoon."

Oh yeah. Then there's that—the absent father.

"Tell him you're getting Internet hookup. He needs to anticipate the expense. Tell him about the deer you saved. He'll enjoy that."

"You handle it, Mom. I don't want to talk to him."

"Kenzie, we've been over this. Your dad loves you. He cares about what's going on in your life."

"If he cares so much, why'd he leave?"

"He didn't leave because he doesn't care about you. What happened was between—"

"Mom, I know what happened. I don't want to talk to him." *And how can you after his betrayal?*

After a lunch during which she and her mom practiced polite, meaningless, and impersonal conversation, Kenzie spent the rest of the afternoon unpacking and setting up her computer. Her mind reeled. She had to find the poacher and stop the slaughter. She needed a plan before she talked to Angelo.

As she opened boxes, she uncovered memories that held her hostage. Photos of friends and Scruffy, trophies from swim meets and softball tournaments. All scattered on her bed like damning evidence. *Deserter!* She pulled a rumpled St. Joe's uniform skirt from the bottom of the last box. Held it in her lap and picked lint from its pleats. How she'd hated these things, yet she'd give anything to be bitching about them this school year. She pitched the skirt into the trash, then put the photos and trophies away on her shelves. If only it were as easy to put away the killer. *Damning evidence.* That's what she had to uncover on him.

Hours later, she accessed the Internet and breathed a sigh of relief. Hello, civilization! Being cell-less was close to death. She would die if she didn't get one for her birthday. But she had weeks to go with no talking, only tapping. She had so much to tell. Where to start? At the beginning. Start with Molly. No. Who'd believe her? Adorable Angelo. No. They'd ask how she met him. Embarrassing. *I'm baaack*, was good enough. Save the details.

Details. Evidence. How could she find any when she didn't know much about the territory or the victims? Study the refuge and the habits of the deer. Hit that scientists' Web site Mike had mentioned. The one about the Key deer project. What was its address? Time to search. She typed in *Key deer*, then punched enter. The first Web site listed was the Key Deer Bar-B-Q and Grill. Gross. Was that someone's idea of a joke? Refine the search. *Tappity tap. Click.* Yes—a listing for the National Key Deer Refuge. *Click.* All history. *Crap.*

Why hadn't she paid more attention to Mike? She tried *Florida Keys.* Tap. Tap. No luck. Why not try endangered animal studies? Studies! Studies are research. She smacked her forehead, punched in the words *Key deer research*, and wandered around until she clicked on a Texas A&M University biology page. Up popped photographs of collared Key deer, statistics about each deer, and a map that tracked their daily movements. Yes!

Beep-beep.

A distant car horn?

Kenzie snapped into the moment when her mother called, "Angelo, what a nice surprise."

Had Angelo found Jigs yesterday? Kenzie rushed to the front porch. Somehow she also had to find out if *his* Jigs was *her* Bronze Man. If so, she had to tell Angelo he was accusing an innocent man. Soon.

Angelo lifted a cooler out of his dad's truck.

"Tell your dad I have some fresh iced tea," her mom called down. "He might welcome it after a day of fishing in this heat."

Angelo spoke to his dad, then walked through the gate alone, carrying a little yellow cooler like a prize. "Hey, Ms. Ryan. Hey, Red! Brought you something." He started up the stairs, stopped near the top, and stared. "Wow, Kenzie, you really are red. Your face and arms are much worse than—"

Don't-you-dare-mention-yesterday blazed from Kenzie's eyes.

"Your legs," he finished. "What happened?"

She scratched her cheeks. "Poisonwood. That's what."

"Oh, man. That's crummy. Guess you got it running along the canal after the dog-deer."

"Ha. Ha." Kenzie lowered her voice. "Thanks, I think."

Kenzie's mom opened the screen door. "Your father won't come up?"

"No, Ms. Ryan. He says it wouldn't be proper before he's washed. He's been on the water all day. Had a good catch too." Angelo grinned as he came in. "He *is* kind of rank."

A man with a head of thick silver hair leaned out of the truck, and a pleasant voice called up. "A rain check, as you say. *Sí, Señora Ryan?*"

"Yes, of course, Mr.—*Señor?*" Still holding the door open, she looked at Angelo. "Oh, for goodness sake. I don't know your last name."

"It's Sanchez." He stepped onto the porch.

Sanchez. Mike was right. Angelo's mom— *dead.* The burning in Kenzie's throat returned. How could he bear it?

"You are welcome any time, *Señor Sanchez.*"

Mr. Sanchez climbed out of the truck and stretched his back before ambling to the gate. He could have been Angelo's grandfather. He smiled up at the porch. *"Mi nombre es Humberto, Señora Ryan.* Call me Humberto."

"Humberto, yes, certainly. And please call me *Maggie.*"

"I would be honored. Now, excuse me, *por favor.*" He trudged with steady and deliberate steps back to his truck as if the earth were a boat on a rolling sea.

Kenzie's mom let the door close. "Let's see what you have in that thing."

"Fresh dolphin. It's awesome any way you cook it."

Angelo held out the cooler, but she made no move to take it. "You'll love it, Ms. Ryan." He lowered the cooler. "It's already cleaned if that's what you're worried about."

Kenzie caught her mom's *What-do-we-do-about-this?* glance.

How was she supposed to know? A death in the family could make people a little crazy, but this made no sense at all.

"Don't you like dolphin?" Angelo shrugged. "No problem." He shuffled his feet and waited.

"Are you nuts, Sharkman? We're horrified that anyone eats Key deer meat. How do you think we feel about dolphin?"

"What's deer meat have to do with fish?"

"Fish?" Kenzie said. "Cold-blooded fish with scales?"

"Sure. It's not like it's Flipper. It's got a Hawaiian sounding name too."

Kenzie's mom raised her eyebrows. "Mahi Mahi?"

"That's it."

"Well, that's a relief!" Her mom took the cooler. "Come on in. Let's put the fish in the fridge."

Angelo removed plastic storage bags of fish from the cooler. "Ms. Ryan, do you have a big bowl?"

"I just unpacked my bowls." She opened a cabinet and handed him one.

He dumped the ice from the cooler into the bowl and placed the fillets on top. "It'll stay fresh longer this way."

"Thank you, Angelo."

"No problem." He picked up his cooler and headed out.

Kenzie sighed. Finally. Now she could get some answers. She followed him to the porch. "So, what happened? Did you find Jigs?"

Angelo's jaws tightened. "He moved his houseboat again. He must know I'm on to him."

"What's he look like, anyway?"

"I've only seen him at a distance. But he's dark, tall, and skinny. Has a long, gray beard like Spanish moss. Why?"

"Just curious." Kenzie followed him down the steps. "What about his dog?"

"Shorter, hairier, no tan."

"Cute, Sharkman. Seriously, you said his dog's big. What else?"

"Big and shaggy. Just an old, brown, mutty-lookin' thing."

Not good. Just what she was afraid of. Angelo was after Bronze Man, who was the wrong man.

"Do you know the dog's name?"

Angelo swung around. "What are you? FBI? No, I don't. The guys at the fish house talk about them both, but *Jigs* is the only name I've heard."

Crap. That didn't help. She still didn't know whose name was *Jigs*—man or dog?

"What's it matter? The point is I didn't find either one of them."

Kenzie swallowed. "Maybe *you* didn't, but I—"

"*Ángel, ¡Vámonos!*"

"Gotta go. Enjoy the fish." Angelo hoisted the cooler on his shoulder and sprinted to the truck.

Chapter 11

Sunday morning on the shady stilt-house porch was peaceful—no voices, horns, or sirens. Only the soft *hoo-hrrooo, hoo-hrrooo* of mourning doves and the coasting bicycle-wheel clicks of palm fronds. Like sitting in a tree house.

Kenzie tried to appreciate the breezy beauty, but she was suffering Angelo-ache. Any response he'd make when she proclaimed him wrong would be unpleasant because, unlike the turtle issue, this time she wouldn't be teasing. His soft brown eyes would harden, and she'd be the reason.

He was hurting over the loss of his mom. His raw emotions were easier to take knowing that, but did she want to upset him more? They'd been getting along so well. *Admit it, girl, you really like him.* Honestly, did she have to tell him that Jigs wasn't the bad guy? She rubbed her forehead. *Yes.* How could they find the real poacher if Angelo focused on Jigs?

"Morning, sweetie."

"Morning, Mom. I didn't know you were up."

"Long enough to brew tea." Her mom placed a tray with a hand-painted pot and cups on the table between the rocking chairs. "You look lost in thought. What's on your mind?"

"Just drifting."

"This is about the time of day you walked Scruffy. I know you miss him."

"I'm deer-watching." She could watch one thing while worrying about something else. *Right?* "I recognize that buck across the street from yesterday. The one with the crooked antler. I also recognized a doe with a twisted mouth. Inbreeding maybe or some other environmental stress."

"Did you learn that on the Internet?"

"Biology class."

Her mom poured Kenzie a cup of tea. "Here you are."

A little herd pranced down the narrow street, antenna-like tails flashing white and proud as if they owned the island. A dog barked, and the lead doe spooked. She fled. The others bolted after her, their hind legs kicking slightly sideways in quirky rabbit fashion. These deer were as surprising and unique as their human neighbors.

Kenzie curled up in the rocking chair, sniffed the comforting tea, and peered across her cup. "Mom, remember when we first got here you made some comment about the ragged, unkempt, and hippie-type people in the grocery store?"

"I did? There were so many unusual characters. That's what I meant."

"Think about Mr. Sanchez."

"It was very thoughtful of him to bring us that fish. I'm a bit nervous about cooking it though."

"Mom, what I mean is—I bet lots of those people were just coming home from work like Mr. Sanchez was yesterday."

"You're right. It's an outdoor life here. I suppose anyone would look pretty ragged after a day under the sun. Even the doctors dress down. Not many jobs require the clean-shaven, suit-and-tie look." She wiggled her bare toes. "I'm beginning to like this casual lifestyle."

"Is that why you've been telling everyone to call you Maggie instead of Margaret?"

"Actually, the girls at the hospital started

calling me Maggie. I like it. It makes me feel like a different person. New life. New name. What do you think?"

New life. New name. Kenzie rocked and sipped. "Not a bad idea. Now, we both have nicknames."

"Yes we do, Miss Red Ryan."

"You heard that, huh?"

"I did, but you don't seem so scarlet today. I haven't noticed you scratching this morning."

Kenzie sat her cup down, then stretched her arms across the table to show her mom.

"Much better."

"I think so. If it's okay, I'm going to ride to the shopping center this morning. I saw a video store there, and I'd like to see what they carry." *And explore more of the murder victims' habitat.*

"You should be all right. If you get an early start and take lots of—"

"I know. I know. Water." Kenzie blinked to keep her eyes from rolling. "And I'll put on sunscreen and wear sunglasses."

Thirty minutes later she was pedaling along Key Deer Boulevard. It sure beat the last trek she'd made on this path. *Uh-oh.* Roadside trouble ahead. Near a Michigan car, a man and a small child were feeding deer from plastic storage bags. Kenzie coasted to a stop and smiled at the

DEER DEATHS
THIS YEAR 49

sunburned mother beside the car. "Hi! The deer are cute, aren't they? They sure like to beg."

"We've never seen such little deer, and they're so tame," the woman said.

"Did you know there's a fine for feeding them? The wildlife officers patrol this road constantly, and they love to hand out $250 tickets. I think they have a running competition." Who cared about the facts? She had their attention.

"Are you serious?" The man collected the snack bags. "Two hundred and fifty dollars would sure put a dent in our vacation fund."

The little girl tugged at her bathing suit. "Mommy, why can't we feed the deer?"

"I guess people food makes them sick, pumpkin."

"It's not about making them sick," Kenzie said. "It's that so many people in cars feed them that they're losing their fear of humans and traffic." And they sure needed to be afraid of humans. One in particular. She looked down at the chocolate-smeared face of the little girl. "You wouldn't want these deer to get hurt, would you?"

The father aimed his camera. "Okay you two, stand real still. I'll get your picture with the deer before we go."

"Hope you enjoy your visit." Kenzie shoved off. If she never caught the poacher, maybe she could save a few deer this way. It was always good to have a backup plan.

Kenzie was as parched as the blackened forest she rode through. But since she'd read about these intentional burns on the refuge Web site, the charred trees were no longer scary. Controlled fires allowed sunlight to reach food plants for the deer, and the burned pines would soon turn green again.

She stopped to sip from her water bottle. *Mmmm. Hydration.*

Knowledge kept her from mentally freaking out. Preparation made the physical difference. Today the exercise felt great. If she rode this path often enough, she'd be fit for softball and swimming, if she quit slacking.

She stowed her water bottle, and mounted her bike, leaned forward, and pumped. Oh yeah. This would get her in shape. Real fast.

Brakes squealed. Tires screeched. Kenzie cringed. Two does and a fawn had darted in front of a pickup. The truck slid to a stop. The deer bounded into the woods near a tall palm tree.

Kenzie gripped both brakes. She sucked in a load of oxygen and forced her heart back in place, then waited for the truck to take off again. Most likely, the driver needed time to calm down.

Finally, it moved. But not forward. It turned, then bounced and rattled after the deer.

Chapter '12'

KENZIE NOTED THE PALM towering above the forest canopy—the spot where the deer had entered the woods. She sped to it. A road. Not much wider than a slash through the woods. She hadn't seen it before. Under the palm at its entrance, screened by low vegetation, stood a rustic cross sculpture. Was there a church back there? She breathed a little easier. Maybe the truck driver was attending worship. One way to find out.

Controlling her bike on the rocky, potholed road was like hanging on to a jackhammer. Riding between the rails of a train track would have been easier. *So walk.* She slowed at a curve, ready to dismount. But the road transformed into a level pea gravel drive. A parked car came into view followed by another and another. Maybe twenty vehicles in all, including the

111

pickup, were tucked wherever there was space among the trees. Organ music drifted through the thicket. Kenzie picked up speed and pedaled rhythmically to a spirited hymn. She arrived at an open-air church, camouflaged by thick woods. So far, not a sign of the deer.

The singing stopped. In the silence that followed, the crunch of her bike tires was as obvious as firecrackers. If only she'd packed her invisibility cloak. Kenzie leaned her bike against a tree, then tiptoed to the rear of the screened structure. Heads turned. Gazes followed her.

The three deer were out back—tearing leaves and red blossoms from the thorny branches of a rambling, woody shrub. They were so close to the building the people in the back row probably heard them munching. Alerted, one deer greeted Kenzie with a stomp of disapproval. The other two raised their heads and stared. Kenzie lowered herself onto a carpet of pine needles and whispered, "Don't worry. I'm a friend. About the best you could have."

The disapproving doe scratched her back while she watched Kenzie, as if feigning nonchalance, yet hoping for a handout. Soon all three deer moved to forage on a bush farther away. No snacks? No point in sticking with this human.

Kenzie scratched her leg. Oh please, the poisonwood wasn't spreading, was it? Ant. She brushed it off her skin. Fearing the possibility of a fire ant nest, she scooted backward and then raised herself onto a log bench under a tiki hut.

With a metallic creak, the screen door opened. Two kids walked toward her.

"Hi," Kenzie whispered. "I hope it's okay for me to be here. I followed those deer."

"Sure. Everybody's welcome at St. Francis." The girl lowered her voice. "We saw you ride in. My mom's real happy you came. You got the deer away from the bougainvillea. Every time she plants one, they kill it."

The boy sat next to Kenzie. "We weren't going to run you off." His words resonated.

"Ted. Shhh."

"We come outside lots of times during the homily." He tried to control the decibel count. "It can be pretty boring."

"Ted, *shhh!*"

The guy had serious volume control issues.

The girl motioned for them to move away from the building. "I'm Jenny Broadneck."

"I'm Ted Shhh. Guess you knew that." He shrugged good-naturedly, then muffled his voice with his hand. "I haven't seen you around. You must be visiting."

If only. "I'm Kenzie Ryan. I moved down here this week from New York, so I haven't met many people."

"We'll fix that," Ted said. "We'll introduce you to Lakisha and Angelo. They're inside."

Her Angelo? How many boys named Angelo could there be on this small island? Kenzie peered through the screened walls. The congregation faced forward, focused on the priest as he walked to the altar. A golden retriever wearing a red bandana padded by his side. "What's with the dog?"

"That's Robin. He's Father Murphy's dog," Jenny said. "He goes everywhere Father goes."

"Robin?" *Why would anyone name a dog after a little red-breasted bird?*

Ted pretended to shoot an arrow from a bow and attempted another whisper. "Like Robin Hood. Sometimes he carries the basket for the offering. It's kind of like he takes money from the rich so Father can give it to the poor."

"Cool." This was Kenzie's kind of church.

Jenny glanced inside. "We'd better go in for communion."

"Hang around." Ted nodded at the tables.

"They'll be loaded with food after Mass."

Kenzie returned to the bench. Angelo attended this church. She could see him every weekend. *Sweet.*

Sounds of sacramental music and communal prayers filtered through the screen walls. It would have all been comforting, but for Sister Martha's voice in her head: *Kenzie Ryan, why aren't you inside? It is not only your duty, but a joyful privilege to participate in Mass.*

Sister, please. Kenzie closed her eyes. *I've only been here four days.* But how could she get Sister Martha out of her head when she was surrounded with the familiar rituals? *Concentrate on the unfamiliar.* This forest. It was unlike any in the north. This could be what Mike called a hammock. Tall pines and towering palms stretched above thick-trunked trees with broad leaves. Dense vines, grasses, and shrub-like palms grew low to the ground. Clusters of what looked like green grapes hung from the branches of short, twisting trees.

Thatched pavilions had been squeezed into a small clearing. Women carried food and drinks to the tables as the screen door flew open and a chorus of "Thanks be to God!" resounded. The congregation spilled out dressed in bright patterns of fish and flowers—a terrestrial reef garden. Half a dozen men wore beards and ponytails, looking pirate-picture perfect. Robin accompanied Father from person to person collecting pats, hugs, and handouts.

Where was Angelo? Wasn't everyone outside by now?

Not quite. Angelo was inside collecting bulletins from the benches. She'd never seen him look so good. Leaning forward as if she'd dropped something, she sniffed her underarms. Why was she always a mess when he showed up? After finishing his task, he headed her way.

Ted checked out the long lunch line, shook his head, and followed Angelo.

"Hey, Red."

"Angelo. Ted and Jenny said you were here."

"Yep, most every Sunday. How'd you find this place?"

"I didn't. The deer did. I was following them."

"Buenos días, Kenzita." Mr. Sanchez surprised her with a big hug. *"Nuestra señorita valiente.* What a nice surprise. Are you here by yourself?"

"Yes, sir."

"Come, have a sandwich. Also we have *postres deliciosos. Mira.*" He pointed to the tables and moved to join the crowd.

"Pastries? Pie! Now that's an idea." Ted U-turned and marched to the dessert table.

When they were alone, Angelo deadpanned, "You better quit following deer or one of these days you're gonna get shot yourself."

He was joking. Wasn't he?

"You guys, wake up! Food." Ted waved a fork at them. "Kenzie, come meet Lakisha."

Angelo led Kenzie to Lakisha. "Lakisha's our anchor," he told Kenzie. "She keeps us from drifting off course."

"Nice to meet you, Kenzie." Lakisha tapped Angelo's shoulder as he edged ahead of them in line. "*Compass*, Angelo, *compass*. Being planted on the bottom of the ocean's a freaky thought."

Kenzie grinned. She could use a compass to navigate this environment.

Soon the three of them had joined Ted and Jenny at a picnic table under one of the tiki huts. Through a mouthful of muffin, Ted mumbled, "Kenzie, what did Mr. Sanchez mean by brave señorita?"

She did her best to look clueless.

Angelo hung his arm over Kenzie's

shoulders.

Easy, girl. Could she keep her heart from soaring?

"This city chick—"

City chick? His sarcasm pierced her soaring heart. It sank, anticipating the spin he'd put on the story.

But Angelo lifted his arm, patted her back, and started over. "This city chick jumped in a canal to save a drowning deer. I saw the whole thing."

He'd given up a chance to diss her good. Kenzie could have melted.

After that everyone had a deer story to share, but all agreed that not one topped Kenzie's. Her accidental heroism made her an immediate member of the group. With all the chatter, it didn't take her long to determine that they'd be going to school together in the fall. Even better, there was an active school swim team and a community softball league.

"Hey, you guys," Lakisha said. "Don't forget today's assignment from Father Murphy." She turned to Kenzie. "We need to plan a community youth project. Something with an environmental theme. Want to help?"

"Why don't you?" Jenny said. "It would be a

great way for you to meet more kids."

"I don't know. Maybe."

"Sounds to me like you were immersed in our environment on your first day here." Ted paused for the appropriate groans. "So, got any ideas for us?"

Kenzie hadn't expected to be put on the spot. Old avoidance techniques washed over her as she escaped to another time, another place. She was back in the drugstore parking lot. "I wish we could stop people from throwing trash all over the place." A tiny deer crept through the woods adjacent to the food table. Reality set in. "But it's the deer I'm worried about."

"Exactly." Angelo said. "The poacher has to be caught. Trap the trapper."

"Yeah, dude." Ted stabbed a cookie with his fork. "Let's set up an island sting."

Jenny finger-strummed the edge of her bulletin. "But, Ted, how can we do that when the cops can't catch him? Nobody knows who it is."

"*I* know." Angelo scowled. "It's the same dude who's robbing lobster traps."

Kenzie caught Angelo's attention and touched a finger to her lips. *Don't say anything.* "Angelo and I are working on that, Jenny. Do you guys have your own computers?"

Angelo stared at her hard, then shook his head. The only *no* in the group.

"Here's the idea. Angelo and I"—Kenzie shot Angelo a look, begging him to play along with her—"are setting up a Web site. I think we can do a lot of things with it. First, we can organize a poster contest. We'll put all the submissions on the Web site for a vote."

Ted held up an imaginary poster. "Help find who's killing the deer and clean up the environment." He pinched two fingers together. "Small print: *Put him away.*"

Angelo turned his back to Kenzie and straddled the bench, flipping that lead weight again. He was not amused.

"We need separate categories," Lakisha said. "Wanted posters and Keep the Keys Clean posters."

"Right," Kenzie said. "But how do I collect the handmade posters?"

"Why not have the posters dropped off here?"

The pastor? How long had he been behind her?

"Father." Lakisha greeted him. "This is Kenzie Ryan."

Father Murphy held out his hand. "Kenzie,

we'd be pleased to have you join us any time, posters or no posters."

"Thank you, Father." *Sister Martha thanks you too.*

He grinned and returned to the refreshment table.

"Okay, you guys," said Lakisha. "Let's think of other ways we can use the Web site to catch the poacher."

"Who needs a computer to catch him?" muttered Angelo.

"Maybe we don't *need* one," Ted said, raising his eyebrows. "But we all live in different parts of the island. We can keep our eyes and ears open and keep each other informed by computer. Then we can see the big picture. Maybe connect the dots."

"For that I'll set up a chat room," Kenzie said. "We can meet there each evening."

Jenny inspected and folded her church bulletin, creasing each fold with a fingernail. "Maybe we can do something after all." She flipped the bulletin, turned it, and studied it once more.

Was she looking for inspiration?

Jenny folded and creased it again, then said, "Maybe we *can* help the police."

"Yep." Ted squinted in spy mode and crouched by Angelo. "If we see a hunter, we can post a description. Big caption: *Have You Seen This Guy or This Truck?*"

Angelo growled. "Truck? Try boat or bike."

He was seething. What was going on?

Ideas buzzed and words swirled.

"Catch litterbugs."

"Form patrols."

"Carry cameras."

"Hang posters."

"Need financing."

Angelo's leg vibrated like a cable in a storm. Why was he so jittery?

Jenny stopped folding. Her bulletin had transformed into an origami bird. "What we need is a big kickoff event."

Kickoff event? Kenzie refocused. "Jenny, you're brilliant. How about a cleanup? The area around the shopping center on Key Deer Boulevard is a mess. A cleanup connects caring for the deer with caring for the environment because trash is a danger for the deer. They root in garbage and swallow junk that injures them."

"It would be all over the news," Ted said. "Reporters love stories about teens who care about the Keys."

"Keys Teens Care!" Kenzie blurted. "That could be our name. What do you think?"

Ted high-fived her.

Jenny waved her creation. "This is great." She covered the bird with her hands. "Not *this*—I mean the plan. We'll get people to donate reward money for information that leads to the capture of the poacher and for poster prizes. My parents belong to the Chamber of Commerce. They'll help."

"Listen." Lakisha motioned everyone close. "We might not want to tell our parents too much about how we're going to be riding around looking for a guy with a gun."

"Okay, so publicly we concentrate on catching litterbugs," Ted said. "What about your parents, Kenzie? Will they be okay with you doing all this?"

Angelo sneered. "Her *parent*. She doesn't talk to her dad."

Kenzie could have smacked him. "Mom would be glad to help." *If I ask.* "And I know how we can get businesses to donate money. If they make a contribution, we'll put their ads on our Web site and link our site to theirs."

"If we want to get anything in the papers

for this week, we need to have the kickoff right away." Lakisha winced. "Could we get it together by Wednesday?"

Angelo slapped the tabletop. "You guys are nuts."

"That's three short days away," Jenny said.

"True," Ted said. "But it's up to us to do most of the work. I can talk to some kids this afternoon."

"Me too. Let's hit our parents with it today while they're all still together." Jenny handed Kenzie her church bulletin and a pencil. "Write down your email. I'll forward it to everyone. We'll let you know what we get done today. The sooner we stop this guy, the better."

Lakisha clapped and cheered. "Go KTC. Keys Teens Care!"

"Okay. We have a plan." Ted elbowed Angelo. "Come on, dude. More food."

Angelo, in fire-drill escape mode, followed.

At the end of the congregational meeting, parents discussed and approved the KTC project. Several agreed to recruit help for Wednesday's kickoff. They'd meet at 8:00 a.m. in the parking lot between the hardware and drug stores. Afterward, they'd host a picnic at the island swimming hole. Volunteers would notify the media and contact businesses for reward donations.

The congregation scattered. Some to clean the kitchen. Some to clean the grounds. Others to go home. Car doors banged. Engines started.

Kenzie was high on adrenaline until Angelo tugged her inside. "Are you crazy?" He put his hands on her shoulders and pressured her into a chair. "What are you doing? I know who the poacher is. You know I do. I just have to find where he anchors, and then I can turn him in myself."

"You think you know, but you're wrong."

"You just moved here about two minutes ago. How can you know anything?"

"I'll tell you how." She sprang off the chair, hands on her hips. "I met Jigs, and he's a very nice man, and his dog is gentle and sweet."

"You met him? Right. When? Where?"

"Yesterday, at the flea market. I had a nice long conversation with him."

Angelo backed away as if he might catch her disease. "*Holy ship*, Red. You *have* lost your mind. Stay away from him. Jigs is a killer and a lowlife lobster thief. And that mutt of his is just as mean."

"Children, children." Father Murphy hurried

toward them. "What is all this about?"

"I'm trying to explain to her that"—Angelo glanced at Father Murphy and softened his tone—"just because someone is nice to her doesn't mean she can trust him."

"But Jigs is a nice man."

"I'm telling you, Jigs is a thief and worse."

"Jigs?" The lines on Father's forehead deepened. "A thief? As far as I know, there's one Jigs on this island, and she's a dog."

Well, at least Father had cleared up her dog/man name confusion.

"A dog?" Angelo's so-superior attitude flared as he sneered at Kenzie. "You had a long conversation with a *dog*?"

Like he'd known Jigs was a dog.

"Yes, Angelo, Jigs is Fisher's dog. Fisher is a sponge fisherman. He's also our church handyman, and I have complete faith in him."

"Are you listening to Father, Sharkman?" Kenzie thrust her chin at him.

Father continued, "I'm surprised they aren't here by now. Fisher is working on some crucial repairs today. Now, what is this all about?"

"No offense, Father," Angelo said, "but I have reason to distrust that man, whatever his name is."

Father Murphy tapped a finger on his lips, then placed his hand on Angelo's shoulder. "My boy, I've heard you recite your commandments. I'd advise you to consider number eight." He peered through the screen and smiled at Robin performing his doggie dance. The retriever wiggled and bounced while his feathery tail wagged with joy. "Perhaps you should give Fisher an opportunity to speak for himself."

Robin began to bark blissfully. Jigs—her leash attached to Fisher's handlebars—raced toward Robin like a sled dog to the finish line. Fisher balanced on his seat, laughing as she dragged the wobbling bike behind her.

Chapter 13

FATHER MURPHY WALKED OUT to greet Fisher. Kenzie followed. Angelo retreated through the back door.

Fisher unsnapped Jigs' leash, freeing her to leap all over Robin. When he saw Kenzie, deep creases framed his eyes. "What a welcome surprise. Greetings mysterious lady of the flea market."

"So, you two *have* met."

"Father Murphy, this young lady saved Jigs' life. Had she not, the loss would have been devastating to me." In their enthusiasm the two dogs bumped into Fisher's leg. "And to Robin." He chuckled. "However, in all the excitement, she neglected to introduce herself."

Had she been so busy trying to figure out who he was that she hadn't told him who she was? "I'm Kenzie Ryan. I'm sorry I didn't tell you my name. The thing is I wasn't sure of *your* name until Father Murphy told me. I thought you were Jigs."

Fisher laughed, his agile body shaking like a marionette. "Many people maintain an erroneous impression of me, but this may be the first time I have been accused of being a dog."

Kenzie's face flushed. "But that's not what I meant."

"Of course it was not." Fisher regained his composure. "My apologies. 'Twas a shallow jest on my part."

Nothing was shallow, though, about Fisher's warm expression or his rich, deep voice.

Kenzie relaxed.

Father Murphy placed his hand on Fisher's back and eased him forward. "Our new neighbor has made a remarkable first impression on many of us. When we have time, I want to hear that entire story. But I have a long list of repairs for you, Fisher. Let's get started." He patted Robin. "You can stay out here with Jigs, boy." Then he motioned for Kenzie to follow. "There are new member pamphlets inside. Please pick one up before you go, Kenzie."

Fisher pulled folded papers out of his pocket.

"Father, if you have time, will you be so kind as to look at these?" He flattened them against his threadbare jeans, then held them out.

"Father Murphy! Excuse me." A breathless lady rushed between the men. "Father, you're needed at the hospital immediately. Mrs. Rivera has taken a turn for the worse."

"Please let the family know I'm on my way." Father Murphy pulled car keys from his pocket. "I'm sorry, Fisher. It looks like our projects have to wait. Look around. Note any needed repairs. There's much to be done, and I'd like to offer you as much of the work as you can handle. Keep an eye on Robin for me," he said, as he headed for his car.

Fisher replaced the papers in his pocket. Shaking his head, he looked up at the roof. "Truly, I do not know where to begin."

"I have to find that pamphlet," Kenzie said. "Maybe someone can help us find Father's repair list too."

"Do not trouble yourself, miss. Father made no list for me. I will figure out what to do. But before you go, may I ask you a question?"

"Sure."

"From what Father Murphy said, you have recently moved to our fair isle."

"Yes, my mother and I arrived Thursday."

"Did you move to Pinewater Estates?"

"Yes."

"In a green Jeep?"

"Yes. How—"

"Miss Kenzie, did you trap a deer in your yard Thursday night?"

"We didn't trap a deer. We *saved* a deer and we were keeping her safe until the wildlife officers could pick her up. That was the point of putting her in the yard. How do you know about that anyway?"

"I will explain. Come, let us move out of the sun."

Fisher led her inside to a bench. He sat and sighed. Kenzie stepped to a bench across the aisle. She perched on its arm, biting her lower lip.

"Miss Kenzie, there are many things I don't understand about people, and perhaps the one that most distresses me is how wasteful they are."

What did this have to do with Molly? *Patience, Kenzie. Patience.* "You're right about that. And they throw their trash all over the place too."

"So true. I utilize nothing disposable on *The Bard*."

"The Bard?"

"My houseboat."

"Oh. That's a good idea." Where was he going with this?

"In addition to reusing my own goods, I recycle the trash of others. I search the neighborhoods for discarded, salvageable items. So much waste. I find many treasures that I can sell or donate to those in need."

"Cool. But what does this have to do with Molly?"

"Molly?"

"That's what I call the little deer."

"Why Molly?"

"She nearly drowned, but she didn't. She's like Unsinkable Molly Brown on the Titanic."

"So, she was trapped in a canal."

Kenzie nodded.

"Just as I feared. It was the poacher's doing. His hound chases deer into canals for sport."

So, a dog *had* chased Molly. Angelo was right. Just wrong about which dog. Wait. She'd seen someone haul garbage cans to the street that evening. Thursday was trash night. "Fisher, were you in Pinewater Estates last Thursday?"

"I was. I follow the trash pickup schedules and make my salvage rounds accordingly. The night Molly was in your yard, I was in your neighborhood. A most unsavory character lurked on your street."

This was it. The break she needed. "Mr. Fisher, did you see who took Molly? Did you see the poacher?"

Chapter '14

FISHER SAT QUIETLY. Outside the screened wall a man swept the sidewalk.

"Did you see him?" Kenzie nearly slid off the arm of the bench.

The sweeper moved on.

"It may well be that I saw the poacher."

"You know who it is! Why haven't you told anyone?"

"I have no proof."

Molly might have been unsinkable, but Kenzie's hope had just drowned.

"More than once we have heard the baying of his deer hound. Jigs knows what that old spotted dog has in mind and draws him off the scent. So it seems we prevent the evil deed rather than witness it."

"I told Angelo that Jigs is a good dog."

"I am, however, beginning to piece things together." Fisher massaged his gnarled hands. "Your little deer was in great danger that night. She would not make a generous meal, but this monster slaughters for no reason. I could not allow that."

Kenzie's hands flew to her forehead, and she jumped to her feet. "You took Molly?"

"Indeed." His eyes sparkled. "I carried her to my boat, then delivered her to the safety of the Maintenance Center. When one knows the channel, it is quite easy."

"Well, one mystery's solved. I'm sure glad I came here before I went to the shopping center." She paced in the aisle. "Why didn't you tell the refuge people?"

"No one was abroad that night. I have had no opportunity since."

"You could have left a note."

Fisher's attention shifted to the papers sticking out of his pocket. "It would have been an appropriate gesture."

Strange answer. Hold on. Was it possible? Yesterday Fisher wasn't interested in the dog book. He didn't read the menu. He didn't know about the coupon. Today he asked Father to read those papers. He seemed educated, spoke so well, so formally. But what else could it be?

"Mr. Fisher?" She sat beside him, her eyes on his pocket.

"Yes, miss?"

"I could read the papers to you."

Fisher stroked and pulled at his beard, as if milking it for an answer. After a few seconds he stood, yanked the chain on the ceiling fan, and then wiped his forehead with his bandana. He returned to the bench and met her gaze. "If we are to be friends, please call me Fisher."

She smiled tentatively. "If you stop calling me *miss*."

His beard twitched, signaling his emerging smile, and he handed her the papers. "Thank you, Kenzie."

She lifted the top fold and placed a finger under the words as she read. "Okay, these words at the top say, *Miami-Dade County Department of Corrections*, and this is a name, *Clancy P. Riddle*."

"Kenzie." Fisher put his hand on the paper. "Mr. Sanchez wants your attention." He retrieved the papers, then walked briskly to the back door.

Kenzie followed. What were those papers about? Where had Fisher found them? "Fisher, I can finish reading. I'm sure he'll wait."

Fisher approached Mr. Sanchez. "It was not my intent to detain you. You were waiting to drive Kenzie to town, were you not? It would be preferable to her riding in the midday sun."

"*Sí.* This is a good idea. Come, Kenzie. Already *Ángel* is at the truck."

Why did Fisher have to mention heat? Now her rash was bugging her. So was her curiosity. "Fisher, it won't take me—"

"Kenzie, go on now. Father Murphy will be back soon. He will take care of this."

Of course. Fisher didn't want Mr. Sanchez to know he couldn't read. "Okay. It was nice to see you again." She rolled her bike to the truck, then Mr. Sanchez loaded it into the bed of the pickup.

Kenzie was squeezed between Angelo and his dad. With every jolt the old truck made, her shoulder touched Angelo's, triggering tingles down her spine. He evil-eyed her every time.

I can't help it, she telepathed. *I can't help it.* Great. She got tingles. He got testy. Why hadn't she just ridden her bike?

Good thing her arms were wedged against her body, restricting the tang of nervous armpits. Fortunately, she had aroma competition.

Though it was neat, the pickup smelled like a combination seafood counter and auto shop. What was wrong with its air conditioning? It was volcano-hot inside. Close to eruption from Angelo's expression.

So-oo if he was going to explode anyway, why not tell him now? "Angelo, it was Fisher who took Molly to the refuge. He said he did it to protect her from the poacher."

Angelo wedged himself against the door. "You fell for that?"

"He's not the bad guy." She tilted her head and telegraphed Angelo a silent message. *So we need to look for someone else. Get it?* "He and Jigs prevent deer from being killed."

"Yeah, right. Regular heroes. Superman and Superdog."

Crud, he was stubborn. Kenzie fumed as he smirked and juggled a plastic box filled with his stupid fishhooks and weights.

"Mr. Sanchez, I don't think Fisher robbed your lobster traps either."

"Perhaps you are right, Kenzie. *Es posible.* I have never been so sure as my *Ángel*." He glanced at Angelo's brooding face.

Kenzie's reward was more of Angelo's pent-up spitfire.

Was he angry because he was wrong or because she'd said so in front of his dad?

Mr. Sanchez parked his truck between a van and a giant travel trailer. He walked to the hardware store, Kenzie went to the video store, and Angelo took off across the parking lot. Kenzie waited just inside the store's glass door to watch. Angelo retreated to the shade of a gumbo-limbo tree. He sagged against its trunk—a benched batter after his third strike. Maybe he'd sit on a fire anthill. A big one.

Kenzie moved from row to row of rental movies until she returned to the entrance. Had she read the blurbs on any of them? She couldn't remember pulling a single one from the shelf. That annoying Angelo-ache distracted her big time.

She stood, resting both hands on the crossbar of the door. How long would the polluted air between them last? Someone needed to clear it. After straightening her back and shoulders, she pushed open the door and joined Angelo.

No sign of a greeting, visual or verbal. Not even a simple, "What'd you find?" or "What's the flick of the week?"

He concentrated on the parking prowess of a driver, then snapped. "So, that creep's not the poacher, huh? What was he doing in that spot where we found the butchered deer? And what was he hiding in his boat?"

"I didn't ask."

"Right. Your computer'll answer those questions."

"Why are you so angry? We have a good plan and lots of help. We'll catch the real poacher. You'll see. Come on, Angelo, tell me what's going on."

"Nothing. Not a thing."

"You're just ticked off because you were wrong about Jigs and Fisher."

"Don't be an idiot."

"We've got a good chance to get this guy now. You should be happy."

"Happy. What's to be happy about?"

"If we get him, the deer killings will stop. Maybe the lobster thefts too."

Angelo sighed. A final fireworks fizzle. "You know what? There's no point to any of this. Let's forget the whole thing. Deer'll die anyway." He picked seeds out of his shoelaces. "They'll die, no matter what we do. No matter how hard we try to save them." His voice trailed off. "Just like people." He flicked the seeds one by one across the grass.

Whoa. This wasn't the time for who was right or wrong. Something else was going on here. Angelo was in real pain. Waiting for him to say more, Kenzie scratched the hard, sandy ground with a twig. The rugged fisherman was gone. A wounded little boy drooped beside her.

She dropped the twig. Moved to touch his arm, but hesitated. Too much? Not enough? He needed to be held, hugged, soothed. She'd known him such a short time. Knew so little about him. How could she ease his grief?

She hung her head and allowed her words to drift to him on a soft breeze. "Hey, Sharkman. I know about your mom."

Angelo clenched his fingers. "So? What's Mom got to do with anything?"

"It's just that I thought— Well, it must be—" Kenzie shrugged. "I don't know."

"That's right. You don't. So back off."

"No." Kenzie retrieved the twig, then threw it at him. "Maybe you should talk about your mom. That way I *would* know something." So much for soothing.

"You want me to talk about my mom. Unreal." He leaped to his feet and glared down at her.

Goodbye little boy.

"You're full of it, Red. What about you? You

don't talk about your dad. You won't even talk *to* him. At least you have him to talk to." He trudged toward the truck, hands deep in his pockets.

Ouch. How could she respond to that? Her dad was out of the game. Three strikes—out. One, he cheated. Two, he deserted. Three, he joined the opposition. Her dad was gone. His choice. Absent, but available. That would all sound ludicrously lame to Angelo. His mom was one hundred percent gone. No choice. Forever.

Chapter 15

ON THE RETURN RIDE, the fishing guide guru's broadcast offered the lone voice in the truck. Angelo's silence was chilling. His fire had turned to ice. At least she wasn't sweating this time.

Now she had two Angelo minefields to maneuver through. His ego and his pain. Were all guys so hard to figure?

When they arrived at the little stilt house, Kenzie's mom convinced Mr. Sanchez to come in for a glass of iced tea. Angelo refused.

"Ángel, la bicicleta, por favor."

Angelo climbed out of the truck. From his expression you'd think he'd swallowed a bad oyster. He leaned Kenzie's bike against the fence and then plopped on the bottom step, wallowing in his big chill. If Kenzie wanted to warm up, she needed to go inside. This with the thermometer registering ninety-two degrees. She stepped around him and followed his dad up the stairs.

With an eye on Kenzie, Mom greeted Mr. Sanchez at the door. "Humberto, I appreciate your bringing Kenzie home. I can see her rash is acting up again."

"It was my pleasure."

"Let me see your face, sweetie." Her mom cupped Kenzie's chin and turned it side to side. "Isn't Angelo coming in?"

"I don't think he likes tea much."

"Is the inflammation bothering you?"

"A little." *But not as much as Angelo.* "I'll go take care of it."

After coating her skin with medicine, Kenzie returned to the living room where her mom was chatting with Mr. Sanchez as if he were newfound family.

"You're right, Humberto. My father was cheerful and tireless. He always loved St. Francis Church and the woods around it. He took pride in taming The *Holy Jungle* as he called it. It's amazing that the two of you worked together on that project."

Angelo's dad knew Grandpa Mackenzie? Now that was something she could talk to Angelo about. Calmly. She just had to get out there and warm him up.

"Isn't that right, honey?"

"Sorry, Mom. What'd you say?"

"I was saying that I forget how small this island is, and, like you, I could have found the church this morning with no problem."

"All I did was follow the deer."

"Divine guidance." Her mom smiled. "Humberto, I could use some guidance cooking your fish. What would you suggest?"

This conversation was going to last for a while. There was time to have one of her own outside. At least try to. Away from parents. "I'm going to take a soda out to Angelo, since he doesn't like tea," Kenzie said, on her way to the kitchen. *Time to melt an ice cube.*

Kenzie took a can from the cabinet and one from the refrigerator, then carried them down the front steps. She rolled the warm one over the back of Angelo's neck. Her fingertips brushed his skin.

He grasped her hand in midroll. "What are you doing?"

"Saving electricity. You'll cool this quicker than the refrigerator."

Was that a teeny grin she saw? A crack in

the ice?

"Here." She set the other can beside him. "This one's already chilled. Trade."

"Thanks." He popped the tab.

"Wow." She counted on her fingers. "That's five words. *One* polite. *All* low-volume. Does that mean you're ready to talk to me now?"

He swigged, then swallowed. "Guess I was a jerk."

"I told you before. You can be full of bee boogers."

Yep. Definitely a grin. He was cracking.

"Another case of mouth before brain." As he sipped, he garbled, "Sorry."

Okay, so he was apologizing to a can. It was still an apology.

"You made a good point though, Sharkman."

He slid over.

She sat beside him.

"What point?"

"My dad. I'm not ready to talk to him. Maybe one day."

"About talking." Angelo wiped his mouth. "Same here. Maybe one day."

In a truce toast Kenzie touched the warm can to his cool one. "Guess what I just learned?

Your dad knew my grandfather."

"No way." He nudged her. "I'll ask Dad about your grandfather. Maybe he can explain where you got your stubborn butt from."

She elbowed him in return. "Look who's talking." The cube had melted. Mission accomplished. "Are you ready to start building our Web site?"

"About that *our* thing. Why'd you tell everyone *we're* doing this?"

"Everyone knows you. Not me. I won't know where or who they're talking about half the time." *And we'll have to communicate. A lot.*

"Cool. You remembered: there's actually stuff you don't know."

"Like I said, Sharkman, 'Look who's talking.' Come on. Are you going to help me or not?"

"Might as well." Angelo tossed his empty can in the recycling bin. "When the guys—"

"Keys Teens Care, you mean."

"Got it." He flashed the thumbs-up sign. "When everyone sends you surveillance reports and pics, we need to be ready. Then you'll see that Fisher's the poacher."

Wrong. You'll see he isn't.

When they opened the front door, the parents were still deep in conversation. "Hey, you two," her mom said. "Too hot out there for you?"

"It *has* warmed up." Kenzie flashed a grin at Angelo. "But this morning at St. Francis I promised I'd help with a cleanup campaign and set up a Web site for their youth group. We're going to start on that now."

"Terrific. I hope the area around the drugstore and shopping center is on your list."

"Absolutely. That's where we're holding the big kickoff."

"This idea is a good one. *Sí,* Maggie?"

"Very good." Wearing an amused expression, Kenzie's mom leaned back in her chair. "So, sweetie. Father Murphy hooked you already. Seems working for St. Francis runs in the family." Kenzie's mom pinched her lips to contain her grin. "Your grandfather must be high-fiving God."

"Kenzie, I said to your mother you remind me much of *tu abuelo,* Patrick. He loved all creatures. Never could I put rake or machete to work unless Patrick first played detective. Always he checked leaf piles, holes in rocks, all places to look for eggs of lizards. So small. Like pearls. Each one he put in cotton to keep safe from snakes and rats." Mr. Sanchez's eyes sparkled as, like a child at play, he wielded an invisible weapon. "Safe also from my machete."

"I forget how little Kenzie knows about her Grandpa Mackenzie," Kenzie's mom said. "My parents moved down here right after she was born."

"Hey, Dad, was her grandfather as stubborn as she is?"

Kenzie poked Angelo. "We've got work to do."

"*Un momentito. Ángel, mañana por la noche,* do you have plans?"

"Nothing special."

"*Bueno.* We eat here. I will show Maggie the way we cook mahi mahi."

"Thank you, Humberto."

"*Sí, ciertamente.* I look forward to it."

"Mom, okay if we use this chair?"

Her mom nodded, so Kenzie and Angelo carried the wicker chair from the living room to the computer in her room.

"We've got to get this site up and running today. Tomorrow the kids will start promising ads in exchange for reward donations. I bet Lakisha and Jenny have already put up posters. Since you don't have a computer at home, you can use mine anytime."

"I had one until the last hurricane. Most of

our electronic stuff got trashed when part of the roof blew off."

"That's suckie."

"*No ship.* But if this lobster season is good, maybe I can replace it."

"Let's hope we stop the lobster poaching *and* the deer killing then." She turned to her desktop and got to work. "Give me a couple minutes to register our site and choose the template, then we'll be good to go."

A short while later, Kenzie was clicking keys and sending the mouse flying across the screen like a bat chasing mosquitoes. As the display flashed, blinked, and evolved, Angelo offered approval and suggestions. "Cool. Awesome. Try this. That'll work. Not there. Here."

"You Internet warriors hungry?"

Mom? Kenzie blinked into reality.

Her mom stood in the doorway. "Just a snack. I know you had something after church."

They saved their work and sped to the kitchen where Kenzie's mom had set out a plate of crackers, cheese, and peanut butter.

"Thanks, Ms. Ryan. I'm starving."

"Well, have at it. You've been working for more than an hour."

"We got a lot done too. Kenzie knows her way

around a computer." Angelo fixed a plate and sat at the counter.

Kenzie sat on the stool across from him.

"Did they teach you web design in school?" he asked.

"Just the basics."

"You know way more than basics. How'd you pick it up? Messing around on the Internet?"

"Not exactly. Mr. Sanchez"—she looked beyond Angelo to where his dad and her mom sat in the living room—"I forgot to thank you for driving me today."

"*De nada, Kenzita. Ahora*, please tell us how you learned so well the computer. I want my *Ángel* to also learn."

Kenzie savored a cheese cracker as if it were her last meal, then sipped her iced tea as if there'd never be another. *Somebody please change the subject.*

Kenzie's mom folded her arms. "Kenzie, Mr. Sanchez asked you a question."

Kenzie swallowed, but her lips didn't leave the glass. "My dad taught me." *Great.* Now *she* was talking to beverages too. She set the glass down.

"You are fortunate to have such a father," Mr. Sanchez said. "With computers, I know nothing. Your father, he works where?"

"In New York." She mumbled to the sound of the ringing phone. Kenzie beat her mother to it. "Mike, hi. What's up?"

Kenzie leaned back in the bar stool as she listened. "Yes, we are. Wednesday. News travels fast around here."

Her mom—all zoned-out and spacey—grinned at the phone and clicked her fingernails on the countertop, spider-like, closer and closer.

"That would be great." Kenzie eyed her mom's hand. "We can use all the help we can get." Nail clicks switched to finger drumming. It was hand over the phone or be attacked. "Okay. Here's Mom."

Her mother took Kenzie's place at the counter, and Mr. Sanchez stood to leave.

"*Gracias, Maggie. Hasta mañana.*" Mr. Sanchez motioned to Angelo. "We have been too long from the fish house."

Kenzie's mom covered the receiver. "Dinner around seven thirty tomorrow. Okay?"

"*Sí, perfecto.*" Mr. Sanchez nodded as they left, but her mom didn't see. Her eyes were closed. "Mike, I don't think I can do it." She rubbed her forehead. "You tell her."

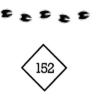

Chapter 16

WHAT WAS UPSETTING MOM so much that she wouldn't tell Kenzie? *And why won't Mike tell me over the phone?* The unthinkable slammed into her brain and she refused to wait. "One of you has to tell me. Now." She grabbed for the phone.

Her mother held it out of reach. "Kenzie, nothing happened to Molly." Then she told Mike she'd handle it, invited him to dinner too, and hung up.

Kenzie stood glued to the floor, waiting. The fact that Molly was safe hadn't relieved the pounding in her head. What had happened?

Her mom slugged half a glass of water as if it would dilute the news to come. "Another deer was killed this afternoon."

Bam. Bam. Bam. Shots fired in Kenzie's

head. Her mind spun like a carnival target.

"Its remains were found on the edge of the Blue Hole. I'm sure the poacher had counted on the gators to destroy all evidence. Amazingly it hadn't been touched."

Ha! Anorexic alligators fool poacher. She giggled at the image. *Holy crap.* Was she losing her mind? How could she find another dead deer funny? *Focus, Kenzie. Process.* The poacher had miscalculated again. Had left evidence. Maybe an identifiable bullet.

"It will be in the paper tomorrow," her mom said. "Mike wanted you to be prepared."

Kenzie whirled for her room.

"Kenzie, wait."

"I'm okay, Mom. I have work to do. I have to finish the Web site. Have to work on the cleanup campaign." *Have to let everyone know what happened.*

Her mailbox held a rundown of the KTC progress for the afternoon. Jenny and Lakisha had already created and attached posters for the Web site. Kenzie briefed the KTC on the latest horror, then told them she was working on the chat room and would send details later.

Because he had no computer, she contacted Angelo on the kitchen phone. No privacy. No convenience. Would her mom ever break down and replace her phone? One drowned cell didn't make her a serial-cell murderer.

Crud. Angelo's phone rolled to voice mail so she left a short message: *Mike called. Another deer was shot today. They found it at the Blue Hole. Maybe we'll learn more tomorrow. He's coming to dinner.*

Kenzie returned to her desktop. By the time she'd successfully set up the KTC chat room, her frustration over the lack of a cell diminished. She drafted a group message, hit *send* and— What? Who? Voices. On the porch. The front door was closed, but someone was talking with Mom out there. Father Murphy? She cracked the door open and grinned. *So, he got you too, Mom.*

"Come on out, sweetie. Father was telling me a bit about the Keys Teens Care project. I told him you'd been working on it most of the afternoon."

"Kenzie, I was serious about you kids meeting at the church whenever you need to. It's a great project. The problem is that litter is an environmental issue that will never go away. It's quite a challenge."

"We'll make ripples," Kenzie said. "By tossing the idea maybe the ripples will make waves."

"A true Mackenzie you are, my dear." Father Murphy stood. "With that positive thought in mind, I'll return to the rectory. I wanted to welcome you, Margaret. I miss Patrick. It will be a blessing to have his family at Mass."

"And a comfort for us to be there, Father."

"Again, I apologize for interrupting your evening. I intended to visit earlier, but I worked with our handyman on building repairs until dark."

When Kenzie returned to her computer, she entered the KTC chat room. Ted—a.k.a. *munchman*—and Lakisha—a.k.a. *misskish*—were already there and had decided who would ride bike patrol in what refuge neighborhood on Monday and Tuesday. Then *designdiva*, Jenny, showed up.

designdiva: I'll have some hard copies for you to scan by tomorrow afternoon, Kenzie.

firedup: Father Murphy was just here. He said we can meet at the church anytime, so that's no problem. Angelo isn't answering his phone. In case he doesn't call back, anybody know how to reach him?

munchman: I can go by the fish house tomorrow, but he may have to work.

firedup: At least try. Ask everyone you know if they saw anything or anybody weird around the Blue Hole today.

designdiva: Can we get together around two?

misskish: Works for me.

munchman: Ditto.

firedup: OK. See you then.

Ted wasn't surprised when Angelo didn't show up at Monday's meeting. "I figured."

"Did we tick him off or something? He was sure in a foul mood yesterday," Lakisha said.

Should she explain? No. They'd all think Angelo's idea about Fisher was ludicrous.

"Cut him some slack, girls." Ted surveyed the space like he might find a forgotten cookie, gave up, and unwrapped a stick of gum. "He's been a little off since his mom died."

For the first fifteen minutes, Kenzie kept hoping he'd show. She tried to listen to Jenny explain who had designed the posters she brought, but her brain couldn't control her anatomy. It was like she'd developed internal antennae with the sole purpose of sensing Angelo signals. His absence left an opening for that familiar ache to creep in.

"Cool, huh?" Jenny handed Kenzie several poster contest entries. "This contest might be harder to judge than we thought."

Kenzie hit fast rewind and caught up. "Not a bad problem. Who's judging?"

"We talked the video store into donating the prize," Ted said. "The manager could judge. Okay, Kish. I can tell you don't like that idea."

"Only because someone might accuse him of playing favorites. Why not have Father Murphy judge? Who's going to question him?"

That was an easy fix, and they moved on to other business. Jenny brought ads from the dive shop and tackle shop. Each store's owner had contributed supplies for the cleanup crews.

"Guys." Lakisha held up both hands. "I almost forgot. I'm working on something special for us."

"Free pizza for the kickoff, right?"

"Wrong. Sorry, Ted."

"Dude. What could be better than that?"

"If I tell you, I might jinx it," Lakisha said.

As for the unspoken search behind the litterbug lookout, no one had seen anyone or anything fishy at the Blue Hole. Just the usual tourists carrying cameras. No weapons. No suspicious dumping. Ted knew a guy who'd been on the observation deck around two o'clock and had seen a couple of locals on the trails, but that was it. His friend would try to track down the locals and question them.

The cleanup kickoff seemed to be on track for a major turnout, but they still had no clue how to expose the poacher. So far the going was smooth for the creep. But the KTC were just starting to toss pebbles. Soon the ripples would start.

Before dinner that evening, Kenzie and Angelo sat shoulder-to-shoulder on the edge of the dock peering into the water, hoping to spot one of the prehistoric-looking tarpon that occasionally swam this far down the canal.

"I'm almost afraid to think about what could be at the bottom of these canals," Kenzie said. "That butcher could be tossing deer into the water like garbage in a dumpster."

"You mean like at the Blue Hole? It almost seems like Fis—the poacher's—*nyah-nyah*-ing someone." He waved his fingers in front of his nose like a mocking child. "Maybe he's PO'd at the law or something."

Kenzie poked her shoulder against his. "You do know Fisher worked at St. Francis all afternoon yesterday, right?"

He bumped her in return. "And you know how close the Blue Hole is to St. Francis, don't you?" Angelo scraped bits of gravel into a pile beside him during the silence that followed his remark. "Sorry I couldn't make it to the KTC meeting this afternoon."

"Your dad needs you. I get that."

Little by little he swept the debris into the water.

Splash.

"I only worked in the morning."

Splash.

"So you could have come. Why didn't you?"

Splat.

"I was busy searching a houseboat."

Chapter 17

"**W**HAT? **Y**OU SEARCHED A HOUSEBOAT? Whose?"

"Whose do you think?"

Kenzie scooted away from him. "When? How? Wait. I don't want to know. I never heard that. It's not even legal."

"Neither's killing and stealing."

"Knock it off, Sharkman." Kenzie clenched her fists until her knuckles were white. "That's bee boogers. Total crap."

"Whoa." He jerked backward. "Down, girl."

She stared into the water, flexing her fingers and breathing long and deep. After a few seconds, she brushed the rest of the loose gravel into the canal, then challenged him. "What's Fisher's motive?"

Angelo looked a bit dazed. Like Scruffy had

after plowing up dozens of mole trails but never catching a single creature.

"Angelo, I know he's innocent."

"Like you knew Molly was a dog?"

"No, like I know what sea turtles eat." She bit her lower lip and practiced deep breathing. "Let's not start this again. I'm going inside."

"Hey, Red," he called. "I didn't find a gun. No gun. Anywhere on board."

She hesitated, almost turned around. That was as close to a *maybe you're right* as she could expect. For now. Whatever was going on between them was making her seasick.

"Humberto sure knows how to grill his fish, doesn't he?" Mike said.

"Mr. Sanchez, Mom, everything was great." Kenzie gathered the empty plates. She reached for Angelo's. "Want to check the KTC site?"

"Sure." He got up. "But the Marlins play tonight. Can we check out the game afterward?"

"Don't forget, you two," Kenzie's mom said. "I picked up a key lime pie on the way home from work."

"Do you mind if we have it while we watch the game?"

"That's fine, sweetie. Bring the pie to the table before you get on the computer. I'll cut it."

"Grab those plates, Angelo. I'll get the pie." They carried the dessert and dishes to the table before heading for the computer.

Angelo stooped beside her as she opened the KTC site. "This looks awesome." He rested his arm on the back of her chair. The fragrance of soap and sea washed over her. If only she could bottle it. "The posters and ads look super," he said. "These trash photos are a good idea. Hey, there's a clear license plate number in that one. That dude tossed an entire bag of garbage out." He leaned in for a closer look. The pressure of his chest against her arm alerted unfamiliar nerves. "Who took that one?" he asked.

"What?" She shivered and straightened her spine.

He stood. "That last picture. Who took it?"

"Oh. I don't know who sent it. But it's an out-of-state car. Chances are it's long gone." She checked her mail. "It looks like no news. Just images. I can post them later."

"Pie time." Angelo headed for the dining room.

The pie and plates remained untouched where they'd placed them. Kenzie's mom relaxed in her chair at the table. "The girls at the hospital were talking about hurricane preparations today, and I realized our shutters need repair. Humberto, do you know the handyman who works at St. Francis?"

Kenzie gave Angelo a lock-your-lips squint. "Mom, why don't I serve the pie?" Maybe dessert would distract him.

"Could he do the work?" her mom asked. "If Father Murphy trusts him, I'm certain I can."

As Kenzie prepared the plates, Angelo leaned against the sink, arms crossed. Listening, waiting, smirking.

You're not going to hear what you want to, Sharkman.

Pinning Angelo with his gaze, Mr. Sanchez spoke. "The man is called Fisher. For years Father Murphy has trusted this man. *No sé por qué*—I know no reason you should not also. Fisher has lived in these islands longer than anyone I know and before him, his family."

"To the chef." Mike passed the first cut piece to Mr. Sanchez. "Fisher is a hard worker, Maggie. He does a lot of maintenance for us at the refuge. He and I worked together rebuilding deer pens and clearing downed trees after the last hurricane."

"What can you tell me about him?"

Mike glanced into the kitchen and caught Kenzie's eye. He winked. "Nothing, until I am fortified with coffee."

Kenzie brought the pot to the table.

As Mike poured he said, "Humberto, help me out here. Fisher's family, last name Mitchell, were originally wealthy British business folks, right? They came here to invest in a sponge farm."

"*Sí,* but it did not go so well, this sponge farm."

Shaking his head, Angelo took his plate to the far corner where he turned on the television. The conversation wasn't going his way. But Kenzie was all ears and sat down again.

"Right. They lost most everything, so the older Mitchells returned to England, but their son, Fisher's father, stayed and helped construct the Overseas Highway. That's how he earned the money to buy fishing boats, start his business, and build a home."

"What about Fisher's mother?" Kenzie asked.

Mike licked pie filling from his fork. "She toured with a Shakespearean troupe. When you put the British father with the elegant actress mother, you start to understand Fisher."

Mr. Sanchez held his mug for Kenzie's mom to fill. He hesitated, sipped, then said, "In that family also was great tragedy. *Señora* Mitchell so young died. *Y Señor*...everything was lost to him. Boats. Home. *Todo*. Fisher was *un niño pequeño*."

Just a little boy. Kenzie's heart ached. She checked to see if Angelo had heard this. But his back was turned. Ball game on the screen. *Listen up, Sharkman. You and Fisher have something major in common.*

"Good Lord." Kenzie's mom set the coffee pot down with a thud. "What on earth happened?"

"Fisher believes his mother died of malaria. No mosquito control back then. Lots of guessing on his part. He doesn't know for sure why his dad lost everything either. He told me he remembers a brutal hurricane. They lived alone on a tiny island, so there would have been little protection. His dad managed to keep one boat though."

"*Verdad*. It became home to them."

"Home and office," Mike said. "Just the two of them doing whatever it took to get by."

"I won't complain about my life any time soon," Kenzie's mom said. "A man who has worked so hard since childhood—how did he manage time for school?"

"There was no convenient school in the early '40s. He would have had no way to get there anyhow."

"Does this man have a wife, children?"

"Vive solo."

"All alone? What a difficult, sad life."

"You know what, Mom? He worries about how other people live. I think he likes his life, but he *is* a little different."

Angelo broke into coughing fits.

Kenzie fired imaginary darts at his spine.

"You know this man, sweetie?"

"I talked with him yesterday at St. Francis when he came to see Father Murphy. I think you can trust him to do whatever you need around here."

"It's settled then. As soon as I have the finances, he's hired." Kenzie's mom rose and rubbed Kenzie's shoulder. "New lives, like new scenes, call for different characters. Excuse me a minute." And she left the room.

Angelo groaned in sync with the fans on television. "The Marlins don't stand a chance." The background drone of sports announcers clicked off, and he returned to the table. "Mike, do you know what kind of gun killed the Blue

Hole deer? It wasn't reported in the paper."

"A .22 bullet was found in its head. We kept that quiet. We didn't let on how much of the carcass we found. We did report the fact that it wasn't shot at the Blue Hole, so the tourists wouldn't be scared away."

Kenzie winced. "A .22 is long like a rifle, right?"

"In this case, it would be."

"A person couldn't ride around on a bicycle hiding a rifle," she told Angelo.

"What's this about?" Mike said.

Angelo slid his hand halfway down his face and left it there. A wall to hide behind.

Kenzie opened her mouth, hesitated, then wiped her lips, thinking about yesterday when the kids had asked about the deer rescue. Angelo could have made her look idiotic. He didn't. "We've been trying to figure out how the poacher gets around unnoticed," she said. "Guess that eliminates bicycles."

Kenzie's mom returned. "Should I make another pot of coffee?"

The guests declined, thanked her for the hospitality, and rose to leave.

Angelo lagged behind his father, a look on his face that somehow combined shark and sheep.

"Angelo, you and Fisher have a whole lot in—"

"Yeah, I heard. 'Night, Red." He flipped her ponytail as he left.

Before Mike headed out, he whispered something to Kenzie's mom. As he passed Kenzie, he said, "You're going to get a surprise Wednesday. Wait until you see who's coming to the kickoff."

Chapter 18

WHAP. SLAP. Kenzie flailed her way out of a dream. Squadrons of fighter-jet mosquitoes were dive-bombing the KTC. *Thwack. Ouch!* Why was she smacking herself? She sat up, cotton-brained. What had motivated that dream? Oh. Last night's history lesson—pre-mosquito-control—courtesy of Mike and Mr. Sanchez. That's what.

Kenzie checked the clock. Seven-thirty. Tuesday. Her mom was long gone. The bathroom was free. She showered to rinse off the pseudo itching. Images of mosquitoes washed down the drain, replaced with pictures of a small boy listening to his mother read her lines and learning to imitate his father's British accent.

Kenzie toweled off and looked into the mirror, an actress, flirting and posing. She spoke:

"The rain in Spain falls mainly on the plain," enunciating each syllable large and round. To the actress in the mirror, the imagined husband responded, "Quite right, dahling. Just so."

How could Fisher help but act and speak theatrically, growing up with parents like that? But he didn't *grow up* with parents, plural, did he? Just one. And that one lost everything. But a hurricane didn't destroy Fisher's father. Heartbreak did.

The day passed with a jumble of kickoff preparations and task checking. By evening there seemed nothing left to do except worry. Adding to Kenzie's concerns were last night's parting words from Mike. Throughout the day they flickered in her head: *Wait 'til you see who's coming to the kickoff.* By the time she collapsed in bed, his comment had escalated into an aggravating refrain. She analyzed every nuance of his voice. Had he meant a bad *who*? Good *who*? One *who*? Two *whos*? *Geesh.* She sounded like freakin' Dr. Seuss. Her questions drove her even nuttier than Mike's statement. She'd never get to sleep for thinking about all the KTC's potential mistakes, forgotten supplies, possible no shows, brownies—*Brownies?*

Kenzie sniffed. Was Mom baking in the

middle of the night? No way. As if her eyes could reassure her nose, she willed them open. Daylight. Wednesday. The big kickoff was about to begin, and yes, she smelled brownies. She sleep-staggered into the kitchen.

Her mom, wearing shorts and a tank top, lounged at the counter. No hospital scrubs? She was settled with coffee and the paper as if she had hours to kill in an airport.

"Mom, you'll be late for work. What are you doing?" Kenzie eyed the tray of cooling brownies.

"Baking brownies and reading the paper."

"Come on, Mom. It's Wednesday. You have to go to work. New job. Remember?"

"I thought you liked brownies."

"Are you having some kind of a delayed breakdown or something?"

"Honey, I've had two phone calls this morning." She reached up and pushed Kenzie's hair off her forehead. "One from Jenny's mom and one from Lakisha's mom. I didn't even know you knew anyone named Jenny or Lakisha. Between them, I learned how much of this event is your doing. Why didn't you tell me Keys Teens Care was your idea?"

"I don't know. Actually, I'm not sure it was

my idea." Kenzie found a scrunchy on the counter and twisted it around her hair. "It didn't seem important."

"I think it is. I'm proud of you. Why didn't you tell me parents were helping with the campaign? Didn't you think I'd want to?"

"Guess I figured you couldn't. Since you have a new job and all."

"Well, I want to and I can. Several moms have baked treats for the KTC, and we're helping clean up too."

"Cool. Thanks." Now what? If her mom overheard chatter about the poacher project, she'd get all hyper and start the Kenzie Inquisition. Kenzie snitched a brownie.

"Hey, young lady, these aren't for breakfast."

"Oh? What are those dark crumbs I see by your mug?"

"Oh. Well, I had to test them, didn't I?" Her mom wiped the corners of her mouth. "Anyway, this will be a good way for me to make friends here on Big Pine. Most of the women at the hospital live up the Keys."

Kenzie poured a glass of orange juice. "How'd you get off work?"

"It turns out, Lakisha's dad works at the

hospital, and he has some influence with my supervisor. I'll have to work Sunday instead. No problem."

"Good deal."

"Sweetie, did you happen to bookmark the Key West radar loop on your computer yet?"

"Nope, but I can find it in a minute. Why?"

"I heard the weather might go bad on us."

Kenzie finished her juice at the computer. A storm system was, in fact, heading toward the Keys, so they wasted no time getting ready and made an early start.

When they arrived at the shopping center, Father Murphy was set up in the corner of the parking lot, ready to go. He'd placed two long tables with chairs under a royal poinciana tree, on fire with glorious orange blossoms. A six-foot banner, strung from the branches, proclaimed, "Keys Teens Care Kickoff Campaign." A watchful Robin lay panting under the table.

"Maggie, what a pleasant surprise. I didn't think you could join us."

"Now Father, I think you may have instigated this change in my schedule. Seems some members of your congregation happened upon my phone number."

"Persuasive members, I see. Mmm. Put

those gorgeous brownies right here." He tapped the tabletop before him. "The cooler below is full of water if you'd like some later."

Kenzie's mom patted Robin. "Father, it's wonderful that you've given the teens such a worthwhile challenge."

"I assure you, it was all their doing. Now, let me take you around to meet some of the parents."

At intervals along the roadside and surrounding the vast parking lot, volunteers placed rolls of plastic bags, some green, some white. Others distributed turquoise T-shirts with KTC in small white letters near the left shoulder. On the back, *Keys Teens Care* was spelled out along with the slogan, *Please protect our wildlife and keep our islands clean.*

With the surprise T-shirts flying like flags in her upraised hands, Lakisha ran toward the table. She gave one to Kenzie and slipped the other over her own braids. Kenzie removed her ball cap, tugged on the T-shirt, and then rearranged her ponytail and hat.

"Girl, it's a good thing we wore tank tops or we'd cook," Lakisha said. "These are heavy shirts."

"I don't get it." Kenzie looked from her shirt

to the banner. "How'd you get all of this stuff made up so fast?"

"You know what they say about who you know. My dad knows just about everybody on Big Pine."

"Mom said he even got her off work today, which kind of worries me because she'll freak out if she gets wind of our plan to uncover the poacher."

"Nobody's going to talk about that in front of parents. Don't worry."

Three green-and-white sheriff's department cars were stationed at the intersection. The sheriff had been directing cars, but when another officer relieved her, she came brownie begging.

"Sheriff, how'd you find out about all this?" Kenzie asked.

"Chamber of Commerce meeting." She lifted the bill on Kenzie's cap. "I know almost all the kids on the island, but I don't know you. You must be Kenzie Ryan."

"Yes, ma'am. That's me."

"You've gotten everyone energized, kiddo. We rely on our prison work crew to keep the roadsides clean, but they don't work on private property. So, your group is performing a welcome service. The merchants were all eager to support your efforts."

"Hey, Sheriff Clark," Ted called as he helped Jenny drag a bulging trash bag toward a pile behind the tree. "What's up?"

Sheriff Clark halted them with a raised palm and waved Lakisha over. "I'll tell you what better *not* be up. I don't want you kids tailing dangerous people around the refuge."

Kenzie checked to make sure her mom was nowhere close. "We're going to watch for people mistreating deer. You know, like feeding them or throwing garbage where they can get into it."

"And make detailed notes to post on our Web site," said Jenny. "About litterbugs, I mean."

"Maybe take some pictures," added Ted. "Of anybody dumping junk."

"I see. All from a great distance." Sheriff Clark raised her eyebrows. "Isn't that right?"

Lakisha solemnly nodded.

"It's important that you don't do any more than that. No big ideas of trying to stop anyone. Understood?" One by one, she stared the four of them down.

Ted saluted.

"Yes, ma'am." the girls said.

"Sheriff," Kenzie asked, "why are you so worried?"

"Late yesterday a gentleman came by and showed me papers he'd found near a butchered deer." She fixed her gaze on Kenzie. "The gentleman's name is Fisher. I think you know something about this, right?"

"Sort of." Kenzie chewed her lower lip. "But he found them near a dead deer?"

"Those papers belong to a recent parolee from the state prison in the Everglades." She shifted her gun on her hip. "He's a drug runner. We're supposed to think *former*. I don't buy it. Goes by the name of Cuda, and he's one mean dude."

This was huge news. Angelo should hear it. Where was he anyway? "Do you think this guy's the poacher?"

"Could be. He's furious with local laws. He's never been able to build on his property because of refuge regulations. In his mind the deer have taken away his rights."

Motive. This guy had motive. The KTC had to find his property. He was bound to show up there sometime. Stake it out and catch the creep. "Where's his property?"

"No Name."

"So what neighborhood is it *close* to?"

Ted lightly whacked Kenzie's hat. "She told you where it is—No Name."

"I mean it's not on this island, Kenzie. It's on No Name Key. No Name is the small island east of Big Pine Key. But you wouldn't find him there"—she narrowed her eyes—"even if you *were* looking for him. He has no house, so he roams like many homeless men in the Keys. Makes it hard for us to keep tabs on him."

Jenny said, "There're Key deer all over No Name. You'd love it there, Kenzie."

"Okay, I get it. I think there's a map of that island on the Key deer research page. Little hoof prints light up on it to show where the deer travel." Kenzie indicated a plate of cookies. "Sheriff, you should try one of these." She lifted the plate, pitching an I-have-an-idea look to the kids.

"These are almost as good as the brownies." The sheriff licked her fingers.

"Have another one," Kenzie offered.

"I shouldn't." Sheriff Clark reached for one. "But it'll hold me until I can have a real breakfast."

"By the way, do you have a picture of that bad guy?" Kenzie asked.

Sheriff Clark stopped chewing. "I told you kids to stay away from him."

"But, Sheriff," Ted said. "How can we stay

away from him if we don't know what he looks like?"

Excellent catch. Ted could play on her team anytime.

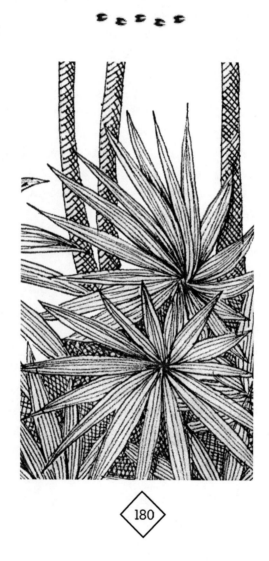

Chapter 19

"I SEE YOUR POINT," Sheriff Clark said. "You should know what he looks like. Come to the station when you can. There's a mug shot on file. One thing. He's acquired a serious facial scar since it was taken." The sheriff touched a finger to the brim of her hat. "See you kids later. Keep up the good work."

"Hey," Ted whispered to Kenzie, "we need a copy of that to put on the Web site."

"Exactly. That's my plan."

Jenny handed Kenzie a pair of work gloves. "Why did Sheriff Clark say you knew something about those papers?"

"Fisher had them at church on Sunday. They came out of his pocket, and I gave them back to him." *Close enough.* "He must have mentioned it to her."

"Come on, guys." Lakisha waved at them to move. "Let's get to work. The clouds are rolling in. We need to do this before the storm hits. We're in charge of this side of the parking lot plus the first stretch of road up to the deer crossing sign."

Kenzie pulled on her gloves. "Why the different colored bags?"

"Green for plastic, glass, and cans. White for everything else," Ted said. "You guys pick up the recyclables. I'll get all the other junk."

Kenzie stared down Key Deer Boulevard. "I thought Angelo would be here by now." She folded her arms in frustration.

"He was," Jenny said. "When we got here, he was stacking full bags on the pile. Then his dad came by and picked him up."

Mr. Sanchez must have needed him after all. But he had worked here first. Maybe she didn't always agree with Angelo. But he was reliable. Stubbornly reliable. His image hovering, she unlaced her folded arms and hugged herself.

She shook off her daydream and got to work. Digging under leaves and pine needles, she stretched far into the underbrush to reach the junk people had tossed away. She collected brown and green beer bottles, soda cans, plastic jugs, even an old flashlight. Her anger mounted in direct proportion to the accumulation of junk in her bag, until she heaved a bottle in the bag with such force that it shattered. *Easy, Kenzie.*

She slurped from her water bottle in an effort to calm herself. Stop thinking so much. She tried to detach her mind from the task and continued down the road. Half a block later, she tugged on a piece of hard plastic, but it was tough to budge. It had been there so long it was buried under layers of dirt and leaves. She pulled until more of the mystery item appeared. An old laundry basket? One more yank. No—a puppy carrier.

Instant images. Detachment dissolved. Kenzie sat beside the carrier, sobbing, swamped with painful memories.

Bee boogers. People were full of it. Dumping anything they no longer needed or were tired of. *Like Dad dumped Mom and me.*

A car stopped next to her. "Hey, honey. You okay?"

She nodded and held up her water bottle. "Taking a break."

The car rolled on.

Kenzie wiped her eyes and crossed the road to work on the edge of the parking lot. She couldn't change her dad, but she could change this little spot of the world. A stoop-poke-crawl rhythm shaped her work. This time she blocked the ghost images that rose from the discards, and her mind wandered to Mike's parting words on Monday night, "Wait until you see who's coming to the kickoff."

He must have meant her mom who was helping Lakisha's mother work the opposite perimeter of the parking lot. The women laughed as they struggled with a heavy bag. Mom was getting her wish. She'd said she needed friends. *Me too, Mom.*

Kenzie scouted the small crowd of workers. Would she have to wait for school to start or had she already met best friend material? A weird hollowness stretched from her stomach to her throat—a New York twinge. Or was Angelo-ache creeping in again?

What would he be up to today after he got off work? He still didn't trust Fisher. He'd said Fisher had no gun onboard his houseboat. Was Angelo going to search someplace else?

Why hadn't Fisher told her where he found those papers? They'd been talking about the poacher before he showed them to her.

Woof! Woof!

Whoa.

"Robin! Slow down, boy. You almost knocked me over." Why was he running away from Father

Murphy?

Yip! Yip!

Silly question. Fisher pedaled toward her with Jigs leading the way. On a milk crate behind Fisher's seat, bags of trash wobbled precariously.

Perfect timing. Kenzie dropped her bag and stepped into the open. "Good morning, Fisher."

"Every morning is good, Kenzie. This one is finer than most. You are engaged in a matter close to my heart. Cleansing the earth is cleansing to the soul. I shall contribute my findings to your collection."

Perfect opening. "Speaking of finding things, why didn't you tell me where you found those papers you showed me?"

Fisher got off his bike and lowered the kickstand. Then he rearranged the bags and squatted down to pet Robin and Jigs. He rubbed Robin's ears. "It would seem you have spoken with the sheriff." He looked up at her. "I know your friend Angelo believes that I am the deer slayer. Do you?"

Not so perfect response. "I don't think you'd kill anything that wasn't a fish. But why didn't you take the papers to the sheriff in the first place? They were evidence."

"I should have done so." He spoke to the dogs. "We have agreed to trust her, have we not?" Jigs and Robin rubbed against his legs, wagging their tails. "I was afraid of what else the authorities might find near the site. I feared I would be suspect."

"That doesn't make sense. Why would those papers make you a suspect?"

"I shall clarify. You see, I found my own knife by the deer."

"Your knife?"

"Imagine. If someone had planted my knife, what else might he have placed there or at other crime scenes?" Fisher winced as he stood. His proud stance wilted. Age and struggle a heavy weight upon him. "I did not know it was stolen, though I knew it was missing. It is not uncommon to lose items. Things have a way of going overboard when one least expects it."

"Wow." Kenzie removed her gloves and scratched Jigs' ears. "You're right. It could have looked like you did it."

"So, you *do* see. I was most careful in handling the knife. I picked it up and protected it with my bandana. While considering how to convince the sheriff of the facts, I kept it so wrapped. The few words you read told me I had what I needed. As soon as I finished work at the church, I took the papers and the knife to Sheriff Clark."

"Did she find fingerprints on it?"

"She did. Both mine and—"

"Cuda's," Kenzie said.

"Whose I know not. Only that there were others."

"See, you were worried all that time for nothing."

"Perhaps. There is still your friend."

Holy ship. Other fingerprints. Angelo'd been on Fisher's boat yesterday.

Chapter 20

WHAT IF THE POLICE IDENTIFIED Angelo's fingerprints on Fisher's knife? Many people had heard Angelo tag Fisher a poacher, and he'd often said he'd seen Fisher flee the scene of that butchered deer. Someone could make the case that Angelo was framing Fisher.

Angelo'd also been there when she'd found a butchered deer. What if the police accused Angelo of poaching? Then they'd say he had a motive to frame Fisher. Ridiculous. They'd have to prove he'd stolen Fisher's knife. No way. Angelo had been—

Where had he been? When did Fisher find his knife? Truth was, even if she knew when Fisher found it, she couldn't answer where Angelo had been. He was hard to pin down. Fishing. Working. Boating. Searching for Fisher.

One thought followed another. All going either no place or the wrong place. *Stop it, Kenzie.* Eyes closed, she massaged her temples. She had to talk to Angelo.

"Kenzie, lass," Fisher said. "What troubles you?"

"A little dizzy. I guess it's the sun."

"Shall I see you to the shade? No need to worry about the sun much longer. I will drop off my load and bid you *adieu*. I must depart before the weather turns." Fisher pushed his bike toward the spreading poinciana tree. As she followed Fisher, Kenzie counted dozens of garbage bags around the parking lot perimeter and on its center islands.

"Morning, Kenzie." Mike appeared beside her. "Let's round up the gang. I've got something you'll want to hear." He pinched his fingers to his lips, whistled, and waved everybody to him.

Everybody, but her mother. Kenzie scanned the lot until she saw the Jeep. Mom. In the car with the visor down. Makeup-medic on duty. Unlike Kenzie, she'd noticed Mike's official truck arrive.

When he'd gathered about twenty people, Mike explained that he'd seen a Miami news crew at the Dolphin Research Center.

Father Murphy stood near the front of the group. "What brought them all the way down here?"

"They're doing a story on the dolphins that beached near Marathon. While they were filming, someone informed them about this cleanup campaign. The station wants to alter the perception that it always portrays teens as juvenile delinquents. So they're looking for upbeat stories, and the crew's headed our way. Seems our KTC group is perfect for their series. I expect them any minute."

"Awesome," Ted said.

Father Murphy reached into a box. "It will make a better picture if we're all in uniform. There're more T-shirts for those who aren't already wearing one." He called out sizes and tossed shirts to raised hands.

Kenzie wagged her finger at Mike. "That's what you meant Monday night. You knew. You planned this all along, didn't you?"

"You think?" Mike held her shoulders and turned her toward the square white satellite truck that was rolling into a parking space. On its side it boasted, *WSWR TV Miami*, in huge blue letters.

Around the truck, shoppers swarmed like

ants to a sugar cube, and questions buzzed like bees on flowers.

A cameraman hopped out and a woman carrying a microphone followed. While flipping pages of a small pad, the reporter pushed through the crowd nudging and questioning until a KTC member pointed to Kenzie. The reporter turned, marched over, thrust the microphone in Kenzie's face, and demanded, "Kenzie Ryan, what do you and Keys Teens Care hope to accomplish?"

Kenzie stepped back, her mind a blank. *Great. Kenzie Ryan—airhead, a.k.a Vacuum Brain.* Wait. The problem wasn't with her. The problem was the stupid question. Couldn't the woman read? Look at the T-shirts. Was she blind? There were full-to-bursting trash bags everywhere. What'd she think was in them? Dirty laundry?

Suddenly her mom was beside her. "Go on, sweetie. Tell the lady."

Ted yelled, "Tell her about the garbage."

"Yeah. There's litter along all the roads."

"Beer cans."

"Plastic bags."

Words and ideas flew at Kenzie like wild pitches. She struggled to sort the verbal barrage.

Agitated, the reporter pushed her microphone at Kenzie as if it might break her silence.

Where to start?

"Tell how tourists throw trash out of cars."

"Tell how deer get sick eating roadside junk."

Then, a shout: "DUDE! THE POACHER."

Jolted, Kenzie stared into the camera. "I want to clean up human trash."

The reporter's lips parted, and her eyes searched the air for answers.

"Kenzie means the guy who's killing the deer."

Was that Jenny?

"Yeah, the drug dealer."

That was Ted.

"Drug dealer?" The reporter's eyes lit up. Jackpot. She turned to the cameraman. "Now we've got a real story." They charged forward, firing questions at the crowd.

Half an hour later, with the TV crew gone, trash bags stacked for pickup, and refreshments cleared, volunteers retreated to their vehicles. Cars poured out of the shopping center under an ever-threatening sky. Clouds darkened and billowed upward. Armies of giant mushrooms, brewing thunderous time bombs. Kenzie darted after KTC posters that had ironically turned to litter in the gusting wind.

Her mom pulled up in the Jeep. "Kenzie, get in."

Trees that moments before swayed in the breeze, now thrashed the sky, while leaves and orange poinciana flowers stampeded across the pavement. She fell into the Jeep as the rain pelted down.

Angelo had missed it all. Where was he? What was he doing? He wasn't out at sea in this weather, was he? She leaned her head against the window. "So much for the picnic at the swimming hole."

"Not to worry." Her mom patted her arm. "We're having a party Friday night at our house."

"Honest?"

"Totally true. We'll make it a combo housewarming and KTC party."

"You're the best, Mom."

"Uh-huh. Now what's this about a drug dealer? I don't like the sound of that."

"It's good news, Mom. Sheriff Clark says he's the poacher. That's why Ted said what he did."

"Wonderful. You can stop fretting. The deer slayings will stop now."

If the sheriff's right. And if they catch him.

Kenzie winced at a gunshot crack of lightning. Thunder rolled.

"Sweetie, tomorrow Mike is relocating a deer to an island in the back country. Weather permitting, of course. He thought you might like to go along, and he asked if I'd object. I said it was fine by me. You're to call him if you're interested."

"Cool! I can't wait to get out there." Maybe she'd see why that area was so attractive to Angelo. Maybe she'd even see Angelo. "I'll call him as soon as we get home."

After Kenzie called Mike, she stalked the kitchen phone all afternoon willing Angelo to call. Another desperate day without a cell phone. An internal storm of fear, anger, and frustration threatened to replace the weakening one outside.

Long after the system blew itself out to sea, the sticky evening cooled. While her mom relaxed on the porch, Kenzie gave up waiting and dialed Angelo. No answer. She jammed the receiver in place, leaving no message. Too much to say. He'd recognize the missed call. If he wanted to talk, he'd return it.

Kenzie logged on to the KTC chat room. Time

to catch up on the latest. Kenzie didn't know many of the people who'd contributed photos of litterbugs. Two trucks, one van, and a car had been caught tossing trash out the window. In each case, the license plates were unreadable. Jenny had more posters to send Kenzie, and Lakisha agreed to ask Father Murphy to announce the winner at Friday's party.

Ted sent a picture of a guy walking through the refuge with what he first thought was a rifle, but turned out to be a walking stick. Nobody'd seen a guy with a scarred face, which was all they had to go on. The storm had prevented anyone from riding to the sheriff's office for Cuda's mug shot. Two additional businesses had sent ads for the KTC page: a gas station and a pizza parlor.

As she updated the Web page, Kenzie's eyes burned, and her shoulders ached. She signed off and fell into bed, consumed with visions of emerald islands dotting turquoise water—stepping stones to the Gulf of Mexico. Tomorrow. Her first excursion through the mangrove maze. A boat ride without Angelo, but she had a boatload of questions for him.

Chapter '21'

THE ATMOSPHERE AT SUNRISE was thick and still when they pulled into the refuge center. Kenzie opened her door while the Jeep was still rolling.

"Have fun, sweetie. Remember to reapply sunscreen."

"Mom, relax. I get it." She hopped out, hoisted her backpack over her shoulder, and raced to Molly's pen. Another deer, wearing a radio collar tagged 92, grazed in the pen beside her. A buck. Its antlers mere knobs.

Kenzie touched her face to Molly's fence. "Hey, girl. Looks like you had company last night. Hope you didn't get attached to him. He won't be here long."

Gravel crunched. Mike approached, coffee mug in hand. "Right on time. Your mom said she'd get you here early."

"She works the early shift today."

"Means we can get going before the sun gets so high." He nodded at her pack on the ground. "Do you have everything you need in there?"

"Is this a test?"

"You bet it is. Being prepared on the water can make the difference between life and death. It's serious business."

"Geesh. I don't know who's worse, you or Mom." She unzipped her backpack and opened it for inspection. "Bottled water, sunscreen, hat, towel, and snacks."

"Well done. One thing missing. But I have enough for both of us."

"Enough what?"

"Insect repellent."

Bugs. Right. Why would it be any different on water than on land? Her poisonwood rash had dried to red splotches, but her arms and legs were peppered with mosquito bites. *Ouch.* What bit her? Nothing in sight. *Yikes.* She slapped her neck. "Are there invisible mosquitoes here?"

Mike drained his coffee and mumbled a response into his mug. His arms and shoulders vibrated. His garbled words sounded like *don't-see-'em.*

She scratched her ankle. "No, I don't see them. I don't see what's funny either."

Mike drained his mug and swatted his face. "You're right. It's not funny. Microscopic *no-see-ums* are thick this time of day. At dusk, too, when the wind dies down. Once we get going, you'll be okay."

Kenzie rolled her eyes. No Name Key, no-see-ums, no sense. Where did they come up with these names?

A gray pickup with green and black side stripes and *Law Enforcement* painted across the bumper arrived. The Florida Fish and Wildlife emblem covered its door.

"Morning, Carlos. We have company."

"The girl who saved that little doe?"

"You bet. She's going with us today."

"Good to have you, Kenzie." Carlos stomped his feet. "No-see-ums are vicious this morning. I gassed the boat last night. She's ready to go. Let's move."

Mike put his hand on Kenzie's shoulder. "I want you to understand something. Both deer will be scared."

"Both deer? You're taking Molly too?"

"We are."

"But I'll never see her again. How will I know

if she's okay?"

"This is how." Mike held up a new collar. In addition to a tag numbered 77, it also had a radio transmitter attached to it. "We'll follow her every step."

"She'll be on the Web site?"

He nodded.

Well, that was what she'd hoped for. Kenzie chewed the tip of her ponytail. But she hadn't expected Molly to be taken off Big Pine for it to happen. "Have any deer been shot where they're going?"

"Nope."

Molly would be safe. "Okay then."

"As I was saying, they won't want to come, so we'll have to force them."

"Will they be hurt?"

"Not if we move with confidence and speed so that they've no chance to struggle. If they fight us, they might hurt themselves."

Scruffy's vet had explained this concept to her once. Still she cringed. "Like rodeo cowboys."

Carlos laughed. "Yee-haw! That's us, Florida deer boys. Head 'em up and move 'em out."

Mike went to the office and returned with two canvas cots. He placed one in each cage. Carlos entered the buck's cage, and Mike went into Molly's. With quiet reassurance, slow step by slow step, they herded each deer into a corner. Then they pulled gray blindfolds out of their pockets and covered the deer's eyes. Next, like silent lightning, the officers laid the animals on the ground. In shock and immobile, the deer appeared paralyzed.

As soon as they moved a deer onto its cot, they secured it with a seatbelt-like strap and bound its legs together with loose, soft wrappings. Mike fastened Molly's new transmitter collar around her neck.

"Okay, move 'em out, partner," Carlos said.

Kenzie held the gates open, and the men carried the cots to the dock where they loaded them onto a skiff. Through it all Molly remained deathly still. Was she okay? The tiny doe's oversized ears twitched. A good sign.

Kenzie sat beside Carlos in the back of the boat. Mike perched at the wheel. Even though the boat was several feet longer than Angelo's, with the deer on board, it was a tight fit. Mike kept the outboard throttled down as he maneuvered the boat through twisting, narrow waterways to reach the open channel.

"Carlos, why are you relocating deer?"

"There're too many of them jammed around the people. To stay healthy, they need additional space and food. The herd is starting to show more diseases and defects than we'd like."

"I saw a deer with a deformed antler near my house."

Mike spoke over his shoulder. "That's the kind of thing Carlos means. Your little deer is the right age for what we need out there. It's also time we put a guy on the island." He leaned down and patted the buck's rump. "If we're able to increase the size of the herd in a new location, we'll increase the likelihood that the species will survive. There's also another advantage to spreading the herd throughout the islands. It increases the odds that some deer will make it through even the most devastating hurricane."

"That makes sense." Kenzie was relieved to be out of the no-see-ums and into the fresh sea air, but the sun reflecting off the water was intense even at this hour. She reached behind to retrieve her hat from her backpack and was captivated by the rolling V-shaped wake that trailed behind the boat's propeller. A long, dark form streaked below.

She shrieked, "Shark!" But a snake-like neck popped out of the water. Its beaked head swiveled, playing periscope. A bird.

"Cormorant." Carlos grinned as several more screamed by. They surfaced in unpredictable locations, dove again, often emerging with a fish to flip and swallow. Mike allowed the boat to drift as they watched the birds feed. Finally, the cormorants flapped away, settling on a shoal. There they dried off, spreading their wings wide like a flock of Batman logos.

"Wow. Look at those wings."

Carlos pointed above Kenzie's head. "Think they have big wings? Look up there."

Giant black-and-white birds each with sharp, angled wings and a forked tail sailed toward one of the countless mangrove islands.

"Awesome!"

"Frigate birds. Their wings can span seven feet."

Mike engaged the engine, and they followed the birds to their destination, an island of trees splattered with...paint? The treetops reverberated with squawking, grunting, and screaming birds. White excrement squirted—splat, splat—out of bird after bird. Not paint.

Pelicans plucked and preened, and herons honked. The frigate birds draped their long wings at odd angles over branches, ignoring the racket. But as the boat approached each tree, the birds perched there took flight.

Worse than noisy, the island reeked like a stairway in a city garage. Kenzie's squeamish, land-loving stomach protested. She was more than ready when Mike moved on.

"Look, off the bow. *The Bard*. I wondered where Fisher was anchoring these days. I don't see his blue flats boat. He must be taking advantage of today's clear, calm water. It's a perfect fishing day. It's not always this easy to see sponges. Where's his red runabout? Hope it didn't bust loose."

"Could have," Carlos said. "That was quite a blow yesterday."

Interesting. Fisher owned two small boats. Not only the red runabout Angelo saw.

They neared the houseboat, and Kenzie's stomach lurched again. "What's that smell?"

"Sponges." Carlos grimaced. "See them up in those nets? When they're curing, they stink to high heaven. It's the living tissue decaying. Never anchor downwind of a sponger."

How could Fisher stand it? Once her parents had taken her to Yellowstone Park, where the rotten-egg stink around the geysers and hot springs sickened her. Park employees claimed to be so used to it they didn't notice the odor. Maybe it worked that way for Fisher too.

In the distance a low, flat-bottomed boat appeared.

Mike turned the wheel. "There he is. I'll swing by so we can ask him if he needs us to

report his runabout missing."

Fisher stood on board his blue wooden boat, hands gripping the top of a towering pole well above his head. Over and over he planted the pole on the bay bottom and shoved, propelling the skiff in random directions. Wrapped around his waist was a rope that also wound around the silent outboard motor, enclosing him and it in one continuous circle. By shifting his body, he manipulated the rudder on the engine and guided the boat, hands free for sponging.

They drew near his boat, and Fisher plunged his pole again. But instead of pushing off, he lifted it and dumped a dripping sponge onto his deck. His pushing pole had four curved prongs on its end. A mutant pitchfork.

Molly trembled and raised her head. Mike glanced at her, saluted Fisher, and fed gas to the motor. "We better get this little gal to the island before she gets upset. We'll check with him on the way back." Mike throttled up, and Big Pine Key diminished behind them.

"Now that is a shark." Carlos gestured. "It's a good-sized nurse."

Mike slowed the boat and pointed. "Do you see it, Kenzie?"

She squinted. "The water's so shiny now. It

hurts my eyes. I can't make out much."

Carlos flipped open a plastic box. "Here, switch your sunglasses for these. See if it makes any difference."

"Wow! Yeah. I can see lots better. I thought sharks were gray. That one's reddish brown."

Yikes.

Kenzie hung on as Mike yanked the wheel. The boat swerved, then made a sharp right. Mike killed the engine.

"What was that?" Kenzie asked.

"Shh. Wait," he said.

From behind the boat came a loud, airy *Phuh.* Kenzie caught sight of a large barnacled back, about the size of a garbage can lid, before it disappeared.

"Was that a turtle?"

"Yep," Carlos said. "That old guy's been hanging around this hole for a couple of years. He's pretty far from his buddies, but he seems content here."

"I often wonder what brought him so far inside the reef." Mike lifted his hat and wiped his forehead. "But somehow he found the one spot around that's this deep and staked his claim."

"What kind of turtle is it?"

"Hawksbill," Mike said. "He's found an

abundant food supply here, plenty of sponges, grass, and fish all in one isolated spot."

Phuh.

The turtle surfaced again, right beside the boat, its beautiful mottled shell visible in the clear water.

"Wow. Look at that sharp beak. It's a hawksbill all right." Kenzie couldn't wait to tell Angelo.

Startled, the turtle disappeared into the deep, its hind flippers propelling it downward.

"It's great he's in such a protected place, because hawksbills are the most endangered of the sea turtles." Mike turned the key and started the outboard. "There're still bad guys out there looking to catch them. The good thing is those guys don't come in this far from the Gulf." He hit the gas, and they moved on.

Though the depth of the turtle hole was well over twenty feet, most of the time they were running in water no deeper than four to six feet. Frequent long white streaks marked the dark seagrass bottom, like a jet's smoky line on a blue sky. "What's that?" she called out as they sped over another stripe.

"A scar." Carlos spoke low and harsh. "Damage caused by reckless drivers who have no business boating when they can't read the water."

"Read the water?"

"He means they don't know what the surface texture or water color is telling them." Mike cut the engine. "You see how shallow this water is. It goes from shallow to low to nothing at the drop of a hat, and that's at high tide."

"Yeah, it's weird. It's like I could stand and walk most places."

"You could at low tide. Every boater should take an airplane ride over these islands," he continued. "Then they'd realize how little water we have. They see water, aim the boat, and let her rip, the way they do at home. But they tear up the bottom with their props, and if they run aground, they wind up spending a fortune on towboats."

"Serves them right for destroying the sea grass ecosystem," Carlos said.

"So, tell me. How do you read the water?"

Carlos nodded to a spot in the distance where scores of white birds waded on long spindly legs. "Look for birds standing in it, and go another direction."

Kenzie rolled her eyes.

As they passed over another scar, Carlos

shook his head. "One way to read the water is by its color. Think of this rhyme: *Brown, brown, run aground. White, white, you just might. Green, green, nice and clean.*"

"Okay, cool. So, Mike, why are we running in the blue?"

"Easy one." Mike looked back. "Blue, blue, go on—"

"Through!" All three shouted in unison.

They ran on through the blue until they reached the deer's new island home. While Mike and Carlos released the two deer on an open grassy patch, Kenzie hoped for a welcoming party, but no other deer appeared. Mike assured her that there were several others on the island. "One of the other does is wearing a radio collar too. So you can follow Molly, number 77; the new young buck, number 92; plus the doe, number 85, on the Web site."

The return trip was fast and quiet as they snacked and sipped from their water bottles. Fisher was nowhere in sight, so they couldn't ask him where his red runabout was. But a boat gone missing in water so shallow worried her. What if someone had waded out to Fisher's houseboat? Taken his runabout while he was sponging? What if it hadn't been Fisher at the helm of his boat when Angelo saw the red runabout speed away?

"Mike, do you think Fisher lends people his red boat?"

"Not likely. That's why we were concerned about its being missing."

"Was that the tip of Big Pine we saw near Fisher's houseboat?"

Carlos nodded. "Yep. The northernmost tip. End of the road."

"How deep is it there?"

"No more than three to four feet at low tide. Why?"

"So, it would be easy for someone to wade out there and—"

"That's not a pleasant thought." Carlos wiped his brow. "Not at all."

Chapter 22

THEY HAD NO WAY to contact Fisher until he showed up on shore, or until Carlos or Mike could take a boat out again. But that option would have to wait because both officers had afternoon shore duties.

When they returned to the Refuge Maintenance Center, they unloaded the equipment. Then Carlos left for the office in town.

In the shade of a gumbo-limbo, with its red, peeling bark, Mike and Kenzie finished eating. "Kenzie, should I take you home, or are you interested in riding shotgun on my rounds?"

"What are you going to do?"

"Patrol the refuge roads. We like to maintain a strong, visible presence, let the community see us as often as possible." Mike brushed his mouth free of crumbs and replaced them with a grin. "That way they know we're earning our keep."

Kenzie balled up her trash and zipped it in her backpack. "Are you saying you're responsible for more than the wildlife? You also protect the community?"

"We don't discriminate. Four legs, two legs, wings, or fins—we look after them all. I have to go inside for a minute. Let me know what you decide when I get back."

Mike returned with a holstered gun on his hip. This was a surprising addition to his uniform, but with a maniac out there shooting deer, she was somewhat comforted by it.

"So which is it? Home or the range?"

"Are you going to No Name Key?"

"Yes, ma'am."

"You've got radio-monitored deer there, right?"

He nodded.

"And it's one of the islands mapped on the research Web site, isn't it? Where you can see what the deer are doing?"

"Yep."

"In that case, I'll go with you. I haven't been there yet. Plus, on the way, I can look for other spots that need to be cleaned up." *And Fisher's little red boat.*

In less than thirty minutes, they approached the bridge that connected Big Pine Key with sparsely populated No Name Key. Parked on the shoulder of the road, before the bridge, was an SUV with out-of-state license plates. Standing in front of the open car doors, wearing spotless Key West T-shirts, were three people feeding deer. Several open snack bags lay on the hood of the car.

Mike scratched his head. "You know, they had to have passed twenty *Do Not Feed the Deer* signs." He sighed. "Well, here goes $250 of their vacation money down the drain."

He parked in front of the tourists and walked back to the SUV. Kenzie hopped out of the truck to investigate the bridge and the surrounding water.

Angry shouting fractured her concentration—the SUV man, red-faced and yelling. Like an irate coach, he flailed his hands in the air, disputing Mike's call. A gray-haired woman leaned on the fender, shaking her head. A young woman stood behind the screamer, one hand on the back of her neck, staring at her feet.

The dainty deer trotted away from the chaos.

Kenzie leaned on the concrete rail and stared up and down the channel. No red runabout among the many fishing vessels in either direction. No red skiff docked by the fish-camp cottages hugging the Big Pine shoreline.

Overhead, an osprey's high-pitched cry pierced the air. It hovered, flapping its wings backward to steady itself, like a swimmer treading water. The rapt hunter cocked its banded white head from side to side, marking its meal. A drawn-out *cheep, chee-eep-chireep* signaled the approach of its mate, its weak squealing call unexpected for such a strong, regal predator. A blur dropped from the sky. The hunter plunged and struck.

A chilling scream raised the hair on Kenzie's neck. That was no osprey. It came from No Name Key. Someone, or something, was in excruciating pain.

Kenzie raced toward the sound. Another cry. Off to the left. At the end of the bridge, she followed the shore, stumbling through the thick mangroves that edged the island. Another agonizing wail ripped through the trees. Inland. Her tears pooled. Sweat trickled as if every cell of her body sobbed. She broke out of the woods onto a narrow deer path and stood trembling in the false silence.

Yow-ooll. Oooo. Yow-ooll.

Her every nerve stood at attention. Where was it? What was it? Whimpering. There! Deep in the hammock.

She abandoned the trail and crept through the thick undergrowth until she reached another deer run. Heartbreaking yelps. She edged toward the sound, planting her unsteady feet as the path took a sharp turn. What was she getting into? *Oh, God, no.*

She bit her lip and swallowed her scream.

Chapter 23

TRAPPED. TORTURED. TERRORIZED.

A large, white dog with brown spots.

Kenzie clamped her mouth shut. Her presence increased the creature's fear. Its leg was skewered by rusty shark-like teeth. In agony, it struggled to bite itself free, gnawing its leg, the trap, its leg again.

"Gawd-dang stupid critter!"

Thunderous cursing and crashing in the underbrush drowned out the dog's cries as a furious, bumbling giant rampaged toward them.

"You're supposed to chase the gawd-dang deer into that thing, not step in it your own fool self."

Could that be—? She backed deep into the underbrush.

A filthy, bearded man rifle-chopped out of the trees opposite her. He staggered up to the dog. "You piece of crap." He kicked the helpless animal, lost his balance, and bumbled into a tree.

Holy ship. This guy was seriously bad news.

"You've gone and done it this time." He slurred and hissed like a wild animal. "You ain't gonna be good for nothin' after this. Ah guess Ah'm gonna have to shoot you too."

Cowering, the dog focused its eyes on and off the man in fearful confusion.

Crap. Crap. Crap. He was about to kill his own dog. The crazy man raised his head and sniffed. What? Had he smelled her? *Get real, Kenzie.* Turning his face in her direction, he wiped his nose on his arm. A thin, white scar ran underneath his shabby blond beard. *Cuda!*

A branch cracked.

Where? She hadn't moved.

Cuda's head snapped up. His red eyes narrowed, and he locked them dead-on her hiding place.

He knows. Kenzie trembled as fiercely as the trapped hound.

"Git out here where Ah can see you!" Cuda snarled and tilted his head. He cupped his hand to his ear.

Kenzie froze, convinced he heard her heartbeat.

Steps away, palm fronds rattled. *Angelo!* Kenzie squelched a scream with one hand and pressed the other to her racing heart. He eased out of the thicket like a stealth soldier.

"Stop right there, boy!" Cuda aimed his rifle at Angelo's head. "Less you wanna go out with this useless mutt."

The dog quieted. His attention riveted on the action around him.

"Why would you want to kill that hound or me?" Angelo crossed his arms. "I'm guessing neither one of us'll taste real good."

"She-et, boy, just 'cause you shoot somethin' don't mean you gotta eat it." He rested the rifle against his leg and reached into the back pocket of his camouflage pants. Then he pulled out a flask. His rifle arm relaxed as he guzzled.

Angelo's eyes lasered through the wall of trees surrounding Kenzie. How did he know where she was? He jerked his head several times in the direction of the bridge. The strength of his get-out-of-here concern overwhelmed her.

But no way would she leave Angelo alone with this maniac. She had to do something.

Find a weapon. Anything. A stick, a bottle—

A rock.

This entire island was one huge coral rock. Pieces of it lay all around her, and they were sharp. She'd struck out Slugger Patterson with no problem. How hard could it be to knock down a stinking drunk?

Cuda smacked his lips. "If ya drink enough of this, anything'll go down good." He cackled as if he couldn't wait for a taste of canine-human stew.

Angelo looked toward her again.

She telepathed, *I'm not leaving you.*

With staccato motions, he jerked his head and flicked his hand.

"What's with you, boy? 'Skeetas botherin' ya?" Cuda cackled again. "Ah kin fix that." Fumbling, he returned the flask to his pocket, then raised the rifle. Its muzzle traced ragged figure eights in the air between him and Angelo.

Angelo stepped up his furtive signals and mouthed, "Go!"

If he didn't settle down, he would blow her cover.

Snap out of it, Kenzie. Find the rock. She visually sorted the stones at her feet. Too light.

Too small. Too heavy. That one. The perfect, jagged coral rock. She scooped it up, moved into the open, and zoom. She pitched the fastball of her life.

Bull's-eye!

Cuda staggered, dropped the rifle, then clutched his bleeding head. "What was that?" Bobble-headed, he blinked at Kenzie. "Another kid." Curses pelted the air.

Angelo seized the gun. "Great shot, Red!" He glared at Cuda. "Sit down before I put you out of your misery, you slimy barracuda." His voice was far steadier than his hands.

Cuda collapsed in a heap, cursing and emitting long, putrid burps.

Angelo rushed to Kenzie. He rested his arms on her shoulders, unbalancing her with the gun's weight and his nearness. Then he leaned so close she could count the soft whiskers on his upper lip. Smell his salty sweat.

"Red, I was so— You're— That was amazing." He handed her the rifle. "Hold this. I need two hands."

So close. She sighed.

Hopefully, Cuda was too far out of it to notice how much she and Angelo trembled.

"Okay, creep. I want that bottle." Angelo

motioned to Cuda. "Toss it over here."

"E-ew, Angelo. Why do you want that stuff?"

"Yeah, kid. Why?" Cuda curled his lip. "It's good. But you ain't man enough to drink it."

"Give me the bottle." Angelo held out a hand and whispered to Kenzie, "I don't want him to have another weapon."

"Good thinkin', kid." Cuda yanked the bottle from his pocket and raised it high.

Bang! Kenzie fired the rifle into the air and flinched.

Cuda jerked backwards and dropped the bottle.

The dog yelped.

"You know, Red, you catch on quick for a city girl."

"Hold it! Hands in the air!"

Mike!

"Freeze!" Mike charged out of the trees, gun in hand. "What the— What's going on here? You kids all right?"

They nodded.

"Kenzie, give me that thing." Mike ejected the spent casing, then verified that the barrel was empty. "The fool trapped his own dog. Poor creature." He trained his gun on Cuda, while he approached the quivering hound. Its whimper transformed to a low growl. "Okay, fella. I hear you."

He backed off. "I'll need reinforcements and tranquilizers before I can free him."

Cuda lay crumpled against a tree. "Don't nobody care 'bout me? Mah head hurts."

"What's wrong with him?" Mike gestured with his pistol.

Angelo held up the bottle. "Too much of this. Oh, and Kenzie practically knocked him out."

"She what?"

"I hit him with a rock."

"You should've seen her." Angelo rolled his fist against his palm like a pitcher on the mound. "Looked like old news clips of Nolan Ryan."

"You two could have been killed." Mike's gaze was so piercing that his fearful pain sizzled Kenzie's spine. "You had no business taking off like that. What were you thinking?"

What could she say? *I'm sorry* wouldn't begin to cut it. While she rode with him, Mike was responsible for her. He had every right to be furious. Cuda hadn't killed her, but Mike was close to it. If he didn't, her mom would.

Mike pulled out his phone. "Poacher in custody. No Name Key. Send tranquilizers and backup."

Kenzie glanced at Angelo and braced herself for whatever Mike-storm would follow.

But Mike directed his anger at Cuda. Mumbling words Kenzie could only guess at, he yanked the poacher away from the tree, jerked Cuda's arms behind his back, and cuffed him.

"Hey, Ossifer," Cuda slurred. "These things are tight."

Mike hauled him upright. "You whining son of a...gun. I ought to slap them on your neck. Collar you with them, dog that you are."

Mike answered his phone. "Park by the bridge and follow the central deer run."

Minutes later Carlos arrived with the tranquilizer gun, eliciting more growls and howls from the dog. Carlos raised an eyebrow. "Didn't expect to see you again so soon, Kenzie. Glad you kids are all right."

He sedated the hound, then waited, glaring at Cuda until it took effect. "If you weren't cuffed, I'd make you pull this medieval contraption apart and hope it took your hand off in the process."

Carlos lifted the inert dog and followed as Mike forced a staggering Cuda along the path. Angelo and Kenzie trailed behind. They traded amused glances each time Cuda stumbled and

Mike backed off, allowing the poacher to stagger until he righted himself.

When they reached the refuge patrol car, Carlos placed the hound on the front seat. Mike shoved Cuda in the back. "You'd best cooperate. Otherwise, the sheriff will toss you in a cell with this poor abused hound the instant it's fit to exact revenge."

Chapter 24

Cuda had been arrested more than twenty-four hours ago, and Kenzie still couldn't believe all that had occurred before his capture or all that hadn't happened after. Not once did she hear *You never stop to think about consequences.* Not once did she sit through a *what-if* lecture. From Mike or Mom. *Please, guys,* she thought, *don't start in front of all these people tonight.*

Mom had been distracted by the party. Kenzie'd encouraged that focus by operating in model-daughter mode. As of yesterday morning, stacks of unpacked boxes still jammed the house. She'd tackled them as soon as a frighteningly silent Mike dropped her off, and she'd finished the job before her mom had gotten home today. Tonight they needed every square foot of space.

So many new friends were here: Angelo, his

dad, Mike, Fisher, the KTC members, and many of their parents. Father Murphy was searching for a place to hang the winning poster. The little stilt house was crammed. Guests spilled onto both porches and into the yard below. How had they connected with so many people in one week?

Uh-oh. Her mom didn't look pleased. What was Mike telling her?

When Kenzie joined the little group clustered around them, Mike winked at her and kept talking. "I tell you, Maggie, I was furious with those two. But what could I say? After all, they'd caught the thieving poacher. They solved the most difficult case I've had in the four years I've worked for the refuge. It was a little embarrassing."

Her mom scratched her temple. "Cuda was a thief as well as a poacher?"

"You bet he was. Right, Dad?" Angelo handed Mr. Sanchez a soda.

"*Es verdad.* Many times my traps were robbed. To dive them is easy. The red boat, waiting above. People would see and think Fisher. *Ángel* sees this red boat, but it is too fast for him. Always I think, Fisher?" He spread his arms and shrugged. "*¿Por qué?* A peaceful man.

He has no reason."

Fisher bowed. "Your confidence honors me."

"*Un buen hombre debe ser siempre respetado.* A good man must always be honored. I am happy we put this problem to rest." He waved a greeting across the room. "Excuse me, *por favor.*"

"So, that is why the red boat was missing from Fisher's houseboat yesterday." Kenzie tapped Mike's arm. "I knew it."

"Yeah, Cuda took it," Angelo said. "But when I followed it, I thought you were in it, Fisher."

"Of course, lad. Why would you not?"

"I found it beached at a campsite on No Name." He tossed an arm over Kenzie's shoulders.

Ouch. He'd caught her hair. She bit her lip and leaned into him...to ease the pain.

"That's when I noticed Fastball Ryan here running across the bridge."

Her mom fixed Kenzie with a stern one-hundred-word stare.

"I figured you were checking out those howls." Angelo gave Kenzie a knowing smile. "But you weren't easy to find. You're turning into a great spy." His arm tightened.

A hug!

Mike threatened her with his soda can. "You should have waited for me."

Angelo shifted his position and stuck both hands in his pockets.

Well, it was nice while it lasted.

"I was so sure it would be you, Fisher. I feel lousy about that. But Cuda's one sneaky bad a—"

"Indeed, Angelo. He is sly. He framed me quite successfully. My runabout fuel never seemed to transport me as far as it should. It had no leaks, so I suspected someone was tampering with it. Alas, the tides leave no trace of evidence."

"Wish you'd called the refuge. We'd have put out an APB for your boat. Did you have any idea it was the poacher?"

"Not until I found my missing blade. A man like that. Who knows what he might do? After that I never left Jigs at home."

Kenzie was wide eyed. "He—he might have killed her."

"Hey, he can't hurt anyone now." Angelo brushed a finger through Kenzie's hair, then turned to Fisher. "You know, I saw your red boat in a canal over here right after we found a dead deer. Was it really you that time?"

Kenzie's mom gasped. "You two found a dead deer? When did that happen?"

"Don't worry, Mom." Kenzie patted her

mother's back. "I'll fill you in later." This time she was rewarded with a *two*-hundred-word glare.

Fisher stroked his beard. "Friday?"

Angelo nodded.

"A most auspicious day. Anticipating an afternoon of land-bound labor, I set the morning aside to search for the mother lode of snapper. Instead I found the devil's dregs, thanks to Jigs. She became agitated, plunged into the canal, scrambled up the boat ramp, and then raced off like the wind."

"I've seen her behave like that before." Kenzie giggled.

"Seen what? Where?"

"Mom, please. It's a long story. Wait a second."

"I'll give you five minutes, young lady. That's it."

Fisher's eyes were bright with mischief. "That you have, lass, but this time Jigs was not playing. She'd sensed that old hound and led me to the same carcass I presume you found. She must have frightened Cuda away, as he left rather carelessly. He'd dropped my knife next to the remains, which I'm certain was his intention. I found the parole papers nearby. Those were an accidental loss."

"Knife?" Kenzie's mom pressed a hand on her chest as if it might rupture. "Parole papers? Mike, do you know what they're talking about?"

He shrugged and developed a deep fascination with floor tiles.

"All's well that ends well, Ms. Ryan." Fisher held up a hand as if to ward off her fear before he finished his story. "After I retrieved my knife, Jigs picked up the scent and was off once more. When I stopped to gather those papers, I lost sight of her. Fortunately, when I returned to the boat, she was waiting onboard in the shade of the tarp, and I hastened to work."

"Tarp?" Angelo slumped onto a stool, hand over his eyes. "I thought you were hiding something."

"Hiding something? Where? Under my tarp?"

"Well," Kenzie said, "It was the morning after..."

"All this time, lad. You believed I was hiding—"

"Molly. Or some other dead deer." Kenzie shared a sheepish look with Angelo. "We didn't know you'd already taken Molly to the refuge."

"More dead deer talk. Okay, that's it."

Kenzie's mom checked her watch. "Four minutes and counting, daughter dear. I'll be by the cooler."

Angelo's chin sunk to his chest. "I feel like an idiot. Totally." He shook his head, then met Fisher's eyes. "I'm sorry, Fisher, for all the stupid things I said. And thought."

"I accept your apology and thank you for it." Fisher nodded, half bowing. "Thank you for returning my boat as well."

"It was Mike's idea for me to tow it to *The Bard*."

"You could have refused. Your conduct was admirable."

"Hey," Kenzie said. "Enough of the serious stuff. I'm going to find Mom."

Her mom sat on the ice chest tapping her foot. "You have exceeded your five-minute grace period."

"Uh-oh. Then it's good you found the best place to keep your cool."

Her mother's smirking lips twitched, then broke into a smile. She sighed.

"Sorry, Mom. I wasn't watching the time. But I'm here now. Let's find a quiet space inside." As they edged through the people, Kenzie put her arm around her mom. "Thanks for having the party here."

"You're welcome. It's been fun." Her mother piled cushions in a corner of the living room floor, plopped down, then patted the one next to her. "I'm all ears."

✽ ✽ ✽ ✽ ✽

"Good heavens, Kenzie. I don't want to think about how many of our rules you broke. Maybe even laws. I should be irate with you, but I'm too exhausted." She leaned against the wall. "At any rate, all's well that ends well. Fisher's right."

"Fisher and *Shakespeare*."

Why'd Fisher refer to that play? He might have made her mom feel better. But he'd been talking about Kenzie's adventure with Angelo, and his reference to a play about a crazy relationship was unsettling.

Her mom sighed and raised her glass. "What a week. Here's to our new home and our new friends. But, before you get involved in any more adventures, promise me one thing."

"Kenzie," Ted called from the back door. "Come on down."

"Be there in a sec." She helped her mom up off the floor. "Promise you what?"

"To filter the details when you talk to Nana, and from now on leave crime solving to the pros."

"Kenzie, are you coming?" Ted was halfway into the living room when he saw her. "We have a party crasher out here."

"On my way." She headed for the back door, turned around, and grinned at her mother. "Don't worry Mom. Crashing a party's not a crime. Unless it's at the White House."

Chapter 25

WHEN THEY HIT the bottom step, music replaced the indoor buzz of conversation and laughter. Several people Kenzie recognized from the cleanup danced on the concrete parking area under the stilt house. Others chatted with an unfamiliar, cheery man around a table covered with bowls of popcorn, pretzels, and cookies.

Ted dragged Kenzie to the stranger. "Coach, here's ruthless Red Ryan herself."

Coach grinned at Kenzie with Christmas-bonus enthusiasm. "How'd you like to try out for the Big Pine Ospreys?"

"Really?" This guy got down to business in a hurry.

"Yep. We need a replacement pitcher."

"Sure, I'd like that. I pitched for my old school."

"Excellent. From what I hear, you're a natural." Laughing, he threw an imaginary ball across the fence. "I hope you're as accurate with a ball as you are with a rock."

"I can strike out any batter in the box." *Eventually.*

"Good." He shook her hand. "I'm Coach Jackson. I'll sign you up."

"Interesting news, everyone," Father Murphy announced from the top of the steps. "Come on in. Channel 9 is updating the KTC cleanup story with the arrest of the poacher."

His words drew guests to the TV like iron filings to a magnet. After a brief review of KTC's environmental mission, Channel 9 aired clips of Kenzie and Angelo. Then the camera zoomed in on a photo of Cuda's now beardless, scarred face.

The reporter closed by saying, "With the capture of the accused poacher, the members of Keys Teens Care have cleaned up their environment in a dramatic and unexpected way."

When they heard the word *unexpected,* several KTC members exchanged quick grins. Ted coughed into his sleeve.

The anchor's voice queried, "Two questions,

Rick. What happened to the injured deerhound, and what do Kenzie and Angelo plan to do with their reward money?"

"Angelo! We forgot."

Angelo grabbed her hand and squeezed. "Totally."

She stared at her tingling hand—afraid to move.

"Well, Marta," the reporter responded. "The deerhound was treated at the Marathon Veterinary Hospital. He's fine except for a slight limp. But he needs a good home. For adoption information call 1-800-RES-Q-DOG." He paused before adding, "As long as you don't live in the National Key Deer Refuge." He chuckled, pleased with his little joke. "As for the reward money, at this time, we have no information, but we'll continue to follow the story of these Florida Keys green teens."

Lakisha switched off the TV, staring at Angelo and Kenzie like she'd just discovered they were Batman and Robin.

She wasn't the only wide-eyed one.

Jenny broke the silence. "Kenzie, what will you do with the money?"

"I—I don't know." She bit her lip. *Dad's the money brain.*

Ted reached over and high-fived Angelo. "Way to go, dude. What are you thinking?"

"New rods. Maybe a computer. If I knew what kind to get."

Kenzie twirled a piece of her hair. *Dad's a computer genius.*

"What will we do with the KTC Web site now?" Jenny asked. "It was coming together so well."

Kenzie tapped her soda can. "We could spend a lifetime on the litter problem alone. We cleaned up one of many spots that need it on Big Pine Key. Plus there are lots of other islands. You heard the TV, we're part of the green teen movement."

"So now we're Keys Green Teens Care?" Lakisha lifted the hem of her KTC shirt. "Should have picked green instead of turquoise."

Mike picked his way through the kids. He held up his phone. "I just got a call."

It couldn't be. Not another...

"Kenzie, relax. A great call from a *Conch News* reporter. The paper's going to help sponsor your Web site. He also said the paper received an anonymous phone call from someone who'll pay for KTC litter control signs if you get permission to put them up."

"See, Jenny, we can't stop now."

"Your mom wants to see you on the front porch," Mike told Kenzie, then poked Angelo on the shoulder. "You, too."

Lakisha checked the wall clock. "I have to go. This was a blast, Kenzie. Thanks. It was way better than a picnic at the swimming hole. Not so many bugs."

As Kenzie and Angelo followed Mike, they said goodbye to other families who were leaving.

"What's up, Mom?"

Her mother eased the loose hair out of Kenzie's face and kissed her on the forehead. "I know this move's been tough, so I wanted to find you something exceptional for your first birthday in your new home."

"But it's two more weeks until my birthday."

"I know, but tonight's special. I had help coming up with the solution, and I thought it'd be nice if we were together when you got it."

She handed Kenzie a small velvet pouch. "This is one-of-a-kind, as unique as you are, honey."

It wasn't a cell phone. Sigh. *Wait.* She could buy one herself now.

Kenzie loosened the drawstring and pulled out a silver charm on a long, shimmering chain. "A key?"

"Take it to the light, honey."

Kenzie moved under the glow of the porch lamp. A deer and a pine tree formed the key's head. Its toothed edge was engraved with the words *Big Pine Key*. She held it by the chain to enjoy its sparkling spin. On the back. Was that more writing? She stopped it in mid spin. Yes. It read: *Kenzie's Key*. "Awesome."

"I'm glad you like it. Angelo gave me the idea."

"But I was only joking around."

"You may have been." Mike lifted the dangling key for a closer inspection. "But your idea was solid, Angelo." He released the necklace. "You see, Kenzie, Angelo quipped that you should be given some kind of medal, like a key to the city."

"Except Big Pine's an island." Angelo stuffed his hands in his back pocket.

"It's perfect." Kenzie slipped it over her head. She caught Angelo's glance as she wrapped her arms around her mother. And she'd thought this place would be boring. "I love you, Mom. Thank you."

Dog tags jingled as both Robin and Jigs clambered up the steps. Someone opened the screen door, and the barking dogs scrambled in. Kenzie caught their collars. Laughing, she stooped between them and received a double-sloppy face washing.

Father Murphy appeared on the porch. "Patience, Robin, patience."

Fisher followed, scolding Jigs. "You were told to stay, my lady. Were you not?"

Father Murphy whispered in her mom's ear.

"Oh, why not? Though I can't imagine what will be left for her birthday."

"Kenzie," Father Murphy said. "Robin and Jigs also have a surprise for you."

Her mom stooped beside Kenzie. "Honey, we know Scruffy can never be replaced."

"And Jigs will understand if you're not ready." Fisher stroked his dog's head. "Won't you, pretty lady."

Kenzie wrapped her arms around each of the big dogs. *Mom's right.* No dog would ever take Scruffy's place. But there could be another place for a different dog.

"You two sweet, sneaky mutts. You're going to have puppies, aren't you? I can't wait! I've got so much to tell Nana."

"Actually, you don't have to wait."

Jigs and Robin perked their ears at the sound of anxious whimpering.

Her mom went to the door. "I see you found the courage to come up the steps. Now cut that out. No scratching the screen. You need to learn some manners if you're going to live here."

Live here?

When her mom inched the door open, a bundle of energy squeezed inside and raced to Robin and Jigs. The puppy leaped, climbed, and rolled all around, over, and under the two big dogs.

Angelo corralled it, then picked up the wiggling fluffball.

Father Murphy beamed as if he were Santa Claus. "Jigs and Robin's litter was born months ago, and all were adopted. This one was brought to me because the family could not have a dog where they moved. Angelo came up with the solution."

"I can keep him? Is this for real, Mom?"

"As real as it gets."

"I wasn't joking around about this little dude." Angelo stroked and soothed the young dog. "I know you'll take good care of him." He

handed it over.

While Kenzie snuggled the puppy, her wide eyes locked on Angelo's and filled.

"I think she's in shock," Mike said.

"Say something, honey."

Kenzie blinked. "Where's your phone, Mom?"

"Right here. Let me hold the puppy while you call Nana."

"No, I've got him." She took the phone and buried her nose in the scruff of the puppy's neck. Like a mother cradling a newborn, she pushed open the screen door and moved to the bottom step.

Balancing the puppy on her lap, she dialed. The phone in New York rang six times. Then—

An answer.

Breathe, Kenzie. Say something.

"Hi, Dad."

Behind her the step creaked.

Angelo.

He flashed her a thumbs-up grin before he turned and went inside.

AUTHOR'S NOTE

Though the people and events in Island Sting are fictional, Big Pine Key, No Name Key, and the little Key deer are quite real. These miniature deer live side by side with their human neighbors and are as maligned by some citizens as they are revered by others.

The Florida Key deer (*Odocoileus virgiianus clavium*) is the smallest of all white-tailed deer. At their shoulders, adult Key deer are about the same height as a German shepherd dog (24–28 inches). Fawns weigh no more than half a gallon of milk (2–4 pounds) at birth. They do not live in the wild anywhere in the world except the Florida Keys.

Though the Key deer live on several small islands where fresh water is available, the majority of the population live on Big Pine Key and neighboring No Name Key. Of the less than sixteen square miles of Big Pine Key, more than half is protected refuge land.

The earliest known reference to these deer dates back to 1575 and was found in the notes of a shipwrecked Spaniard held captive by the local Indians for seventeen years. Early ship log records indicate that the deer were used for food by natives and sailors.

Settlement came to the islands slowly after centuries of exploration, and hunting continued long into the 1930s and '40s. In the early 1900s hunt clubs were active, and members often used dogs to flush the deer. Though hunting was officially banned in 1939, it wasn't until the hiring of a tough game warden, Jack Watson, in 1946 that the deer population began to rebound.

Watson was fearless. One story tells how he surprised three poachers who sneered at the odds: three to one. Watson brandished his six-shooter and explained their error. "There's six of me."

Another story tells of a rattlesnake bite he received while chasing poachers. He cut out the flesh surrounding the wound, relentlessly tracked the men, and, only after their capture, consulted a doctor.

Watson was a gentleman, though, by family accounts. If he found a poacher's car, he left a polite do-not-return note—before firing bullet holes through its gas tank.

Watson's tough stance on poaching was a reflection of his love and respect for wildlife. He personally cared for old and injured animals, be it an ancient raccoon or a young deer. Locals fondly remember how Watson protected one deer with a broken leg by carrying it in the back seat of his car. Until its recovery, Bucky toured the islands with his head stuck out of Watson's back seat window. He and the game warden frequently visited schools, raising children's awareness of the unique species.

Watson served seventeen years as game warden and effectively put the Florida Key deer population on the road to recovery.

Amazingly, in 1947, around the same time Watson began his battle, eleven-year-old Gary Allen may have begun the official effort to save the endangered Florida Key deer. He wrote letters first to President Truman and then to President Eisenhower expressing his concern about the rapidly dwindling deer population and supporting the designation of protected habitat for the deer. Some people believe this young environmentalist prompted the establishment of the National Key Deer Refuge ten years later in 1957.

The Key deer were officially listed as endangered in 1967. In the 1970s the first study using radio collars on the deer was conducted by Southern Illinois University scientists. From 1999 to 2001, a team from Texas A&M University, led by Dr. Nova Silvy and Dr. Roel Lopez, replicated the original study to determine the overall effect of development on this endangered species and to develop an effective management plan. This team continued to monitor the status of the herd, and in 2008 estimated deer population to be between 600 and 700. To reduce population density and maintain a healthy herd, the National Key Deer Refuge translocates deer to the nearby island habitats of Sugarloaf and Cudjoe.

The Key deer are a rare conservation success story. In the 1940s the deer population was estimated to be less than fifty. After the acquisition of refuge land that began in 1950 and the advent of controlled development, the herd multiplied so effectively that the U.S. Fish & Wildlife Service had to consider reclassification of the species from endangered to threatened. Once classified as threatened, the Key deer remain a species of concern, with federal funds continually allocated for its protection.

Today it is automobiles that cause most fatalities. In an effort to alleviate this problem, two underpasses were completed in 2003, allowing the deer to safely travel from the north side to the south side of US Highway 1.

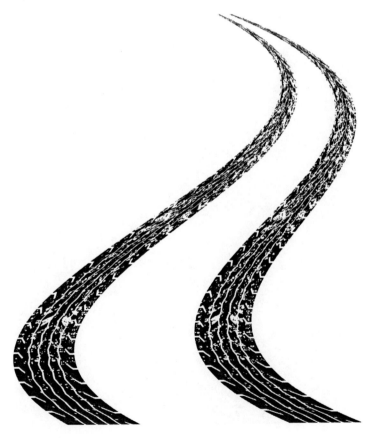

Additional Information

A note regarding the collars worn by Molly and other deer in the story: According to Dr. Roel Lopez of Texas A&M University, the 2006 study of the Key deer has been completed, and, though collars remain on a few Key deer, scientists have no plans to outfit more deer with them. The University's extensive study contributed to what Chad Anderson, biologist at the National Key Deer Refuge, states is, as of the early 2000s, a stable population of this endangered species.

To learn more about the refuge, visit www.fws.gov/nationalkeydeer/. To learn more about the Texas A&M research project visit http://apc.tamu.edu/keydeer/. At both sites you will find photographs of the Key deer and their island habitat. To learn how you can help the Florida Key deer and the other wildlife in the Florida Keys, check out www.favorfloridakeys. com.

The character Whistling Willy who entertains Kenzie at the flea market is based on Whistling Tom Bryant, an amazing entertainer with a three octave range. To enjoy his melodic whistling, visit him at www.whistlingtom.com/.

WHAT EDUCATORS ARE SAYING ABOUT ISLAND STING...

As I read *Island Sting*, I thought, "a green and gritty Nancy Drew." Boys have so many outdoor adventure stories (Gary Paulsen stories), but there are few stories where girls are the ones having adventures and taking chances. Nancy drove around in the roadster, but Kenzie rides her bike straight into danger.

What an exciting story to have a brave girl who isn't afraid of danger and dirt. Kenzie is the anti mean girl.
I like the twinges of romance between Angelo and Kenzie. I like the Website and technology, I like the activism of the kids, and I like a story—which is rare in modern tween fiction—where the adults and young people cooperate and support each other.

Students like to read about teens who make changes and take action to help their environment. They also like happy endings. Island Sting hits all the interests of middle school readers.
Kenzie Ryan—she's green—not mean!

~**Deborah Svenson**
American Association of School Librarians, School Library Media award winner, Texas

ISLAND STING is a rousingly great mystery for all ages. Teachers will love the readability of the book for all grade levels, including elementary, middle, and high schools. Students will love the story cause they'll identify with many of the problems in their lives: moving, divorce, loss, and friendship.

Classes can discover the endangered Key deer and its habitat, biomes, population of endangered species, and ocean science vocabulary. Teachers will love it because they can cover so many of the standards: Science, Math, Language, Vocabulary, and many other subjects.

I recommend a class set so that teachers and students alike can read and experience lessons like one I taught: stream tables to create and really learn about sand bars, barrier islands, tidal pools, herbivores, carnivores (sharks are fun for all ages), and many other skills, standards, and vocabulary in a delightful, suspenseful story.

~**Nancy Rawlinson Schoer**
Teacher of 35 years
Aiken County Teacher of the Year

For ideas on using Island Sting in the classroom:
visit www.BonnieDoerrBooks.com.

STAKEOUT

Bonnie J. Doerr

CHAPTER ONE

KENZIE CALLED IT MURDER.

Most people called it theft.

Nest raids had to end before all the loggerhead hatchlings died. Kenzie must stop them. She'd keep her promise to Old Turtle, if she could get this boat moving again.

Her first mistake? Using Angelo's boat. How could she resist? Ten yards from her house. The perfect transportation. The only transportation.

No one would take her to Turtle Beach. Mom? Too busy. New job. New boyfriend. Angelo? During lobster season, his dad needed him at their fish house. All day. Every day.

She'd heard today's *Turtle-News* report, freaked and took off—without checking the gas—*second* mistake.

She'd been focused on one thing only. Get to Turtle Beach. That's where she'd find evidence to snare the creep stealing endangered sea turtle eggs. Law enforcement may have surrendered, but she'd just begun to fight.

Kenzie kicked the empty gas jug. The boat rocked. The puppy cringed. "I'm not angry at you, Salty." She hugged him, calculating the distance to the beach. Not so far. Swimming was second nature to her. She could probably make it. But what about Salty? She stroked her puppy's head. His ears twitched as he sniffed the air.

Thunder rumbled. *Great* A storm brewed just beyond the island.

She ruffled her puppy's fur. "It's you and me, Salty."

Kenzie scanned the thin white line of sand. No visible help.

Wait. There among the tree line. Something shiny. A metal roof? Ana lived on the beach. Could that be her house? Ana had told her about the loggerheads when they'd met last month. Ana could help find the nests *and* fuel.

Kenzie hadn't planned to look for Ana's house, only the turtle nests. But then, she really didn't have a plan.

So, what now? *Muscle power.* How hard could it be to row a fourteen-foot boat? She'd seen Angelo do it. She turned backwards on the seat, lifted the oars, then fitted them in the oarlocks.

"Maybe we'll get lucky, Salty. Maybe it'll be you and me, plus Ana."

Swinging the rough wooden handles, she glanced behind her, dug the oars into the bay and aimed for the house. Kenzie pulled hard against the water. Row, glide. Drift back. Row, glide. Drift back. The strong current surprised her. The shore was as far away as ever.

How close was the storm? Hard to tell now that the rumbling had stopped. Just minutes ago the blinding-blue sky perched on a horizon of white puffy clouds. Clouds that now billowed with gray. She leaned out from under the Bimini top for a larger view. Above the island, charcoal clouds swelled and piled. No soaring seabirds. No blue. Vast silence. Creepy. Salty curled at Kenzie's feet. His dark eyes shifted, and his nose twitched.

Move it, girl. Arms aching, she rowed on. Only a few months off the swim team and already so weak.

The sky and sea darkened. Reflected sunlight no longer threatened to burn her pale, freckled skin. Good, right? But the wind gusted longer and harder, driving her farther from land. Not good. New York weather didn't change this fast. She rested her head on the oar handles. *I'm doomed.*

Thump.

Kenzie sat up straighter.

Thump. Thump.

What the—?

Salty scrambled to the bow, propped his forepaws on the edge, and then barked. Nonstop.

Kenzie stowed the oars. "Okay. Okay. I get it." Balancing on the gunwale, she moved forward, kneeled, and peered over the side. A sea turtle! Yellow and brown tie-dye patterned shell—hawksbill. Shell bigger than a bicycle tire, small tail—mature female. Awesome.

More than a threatened species. An *endangered* species. This was big news. Turtle

Beach: nest site for loggerheads *and* hawksbills. Kenzie swore at the unknown thief. "You're in *double* trouble now, you creep."

Kenzie glanced toward the beach. A steely curtain of rain charged across the island. Its target? Girl and dog. Goose bumps prickled her skin.

The turtle bumped the boat again. Why wasn't it diving? "Dive, turtle. Dive."

The wall of rain marched closer. The boat rocked harder. Up. Down. *Splash.* Kenzie hung on. What could she do about the turtle now except push it away. Protect it from the battering boat. She reached over the side. *Splat.* Salt water burned her eyes. She shoved. The turtle spun. Faced her. There, caught in its beak-like mouth. A plastic grocery bag. The hawksbill was struggling for air. Choking to death.

On a downward dip, she leaned over the gunwale to grab the bag. No luck. The boat rocked up. She steadied herself and waited. The boat rocked down. She stretched her arm. Not even close. Again and again she tried, but waves rushed one after the other, each pitching her high above the turtle. She'd have to jump in. The boat lifted and slammed down. *Bam.* Her hat flew off as she crashed to the floorboards.

Whining, Salty nosed her leg. If she dove after the turtle, the puppy would follow. Too risky. They'd be battered just like the turtle, and how could they climb back on this wildly rocking boat? Kenzie's heart sank as she stumbled to her seat.

Salty climbed on her lap. Shivering, he clutched her soggy hat between his teeth.

"Good catch, Salty. Good puppy. I can still see the shore. We'll make it. We'll be okay." She tried to believe her words. "Get down, now."

Salty crouched in the bow. She stowed her hat, retied her flapping hair. The temperature plummeted. Stinging rain slashed sideways under the canvas top. The leading wind roared, pushing the turtle farther from the boat. She would stay with it. Her mission was to *save* turtles. No squall would stop her. *I can do this.* She wiped the salt grit off her face, then grabbed the oars.

But she was defenseless against the dark wall of rain. The shore disappeared. The hawksbill had vanished. Which way were they drifting?

Think. Drop anchor. Wait it out. At least there's no lightning.

Kenzie released the oars, reached forward, and found the slippery anchor line. She heaved the anchor overboard. Panicked as the rope slithered off the bow.

No! She'd forgotten to tie it off! She lunged for the vanishing rope. *Thump.* Dip. The boat lurched on a taut line—already fastened to the cleat. *Thank you, Angelo.*

Once anchored, the boat rocked worse than ever. Still, it was better than drifting out to sea. But what would happen to the hawksbill in this storm?

Waves sloshed over the sides. Seawater swirled around Kenzie's feet. Something banged her ankle. Kenzie fished under her seat. Angelo's milk-jug bail. She could work with this.

Scoop. Toss. Scoop. Toss. She'd reduced the buildup by half when light pierced the clouds. The torrent retreated as swiftly as it attacked. The wind and the sea calmed. The sun blazed.

Salty shook himself. Water drops flew. Kenzie hugged the stinky puppy. Her stomach relaxed. "I told you we'd be okay." Salty wriggled loose and barked an alarm across the water.

A few yards away, the hawksbill floated. The bag still trapped in its mouth.

Kenzie pulled anchor. She swung the oars into the settling sea. A few yards from the turtle, she anchored once more. The turtle didn't move. Not a flipper.

Kenzie stripped to her swimsuit, grabbed the loose end of a towline, and leaped overboard.

Be alive. Be alive, turtle. Be alive.

About the Author

Bonnie J. Doerr has been wild about nature from birth. When she was a child Bonnie built huge nests of mowed grass, placed basketball-eggs in them, and became an eagle. She floated, eyes only, above the lake's surface and became an alligator. She collected weeds, seeds, and flowers to arrange on a makeshift fruit and vegetable stand. Then she designed signs to attract buyers for her harvest. Unfortunately, her scribble was legible only to the squirrels, chipmunks, and birds. When she was old enough to traipse alone in the woods and along the lakeshore near the family's mountain cabin in Pennsylvania, she collected worms, tadpoles, newts, and the occasional garter or ring-neck snake for her friends back home. This practice was halted as soon as her parents caught on.

As she played with nature, she also played with words. She gradually learned to put words together for humans, arranging them in works from poetry to news articles. When she was forced to grow up, she attended college and graduate school to become a reading teacher so she could help others have fun with words. Having grown up much more than she would like, she now writes for children. It's her way of playing Peter Pan.

Her novels celebrate caring, involved "green" teens who take action with attitude. When not visiting the fabulous Florida Keys, she lives in a log cabin in North Carolina.

Visit her at **www.BonnieDoerrBooks.com**.

Other exciting releases from Leap Books...

All her parents wanted was for Eryn to live a normal life...

Under My Skin
Judith Graves
ISBN-13 978-1-61603-000-1
ISBN-10 1-61603-000-3

Redgrave had its share of monsters before Eryn moved to town. Mauled pets, missing children. The Delacroix family is taking the blame, but Eryn knows the truth. Something stalks the night. Wade, the police chief's son and Redgrave High's resident hottie, warns her the Delacroix are dangerous. But then so is Eryn--in fact, she's lethal. But she can't help falling for one of the Delacroix boys, dark, brooding--human Alec. And then her world falls apart.

Every woman in the Maxwell family has the gift of sight.

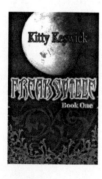

Freaksville
Kitty Keswick
ISBN-13 978-1-61603-001-8
ISBN-10 1-61603-001-1

A talent sixteen-year-old Kasey would gladly give up. Until Kasey has a vision about Josh Johnstone, the foreign exchange student from England. The vision leads her into deep waters...a lead in a play and into the arms of Josh. But Josh, too, has a secret. Something that could put them all in danger. To solve a mystery of a supernatural haunting, they must uncover the secrets of the haunted theater when they are trapped on the night of the full moon.

Coming Soon...

For the Love of Strangers by Jacqueline Horsfall

Darya's journey from a Russian orphanage to a woman's safe house fulfills an ancient prophecy to save a wild species.

I Was a Teenage Alien by Jane Greenhill

In this humorous tale, an alien becomes what she most fears—a teenage Earthling—to save her brother.

Thank you for purchasing this Leap Books publication. For other exciting teen novels, please visit our online bookstore at www.leapbks.com.

For questions or more information contact us at info@leapbks.com

Leap Books
www.leapbks.com